SUCCUBUS MISSION

THE (UN)LUCKY SUCCUBUS

L.L. FROST

SUCCUBUS MISSION

The (un)Lucky Succubus Book 3

Copyright © 2018 by L.L. Frost

All rights reserved. No part of this publication may be reproduced, distributed, or transmitted in any form or by any means, including photocopying, recording, or other electronic or mechanical methods, without the prior written permission of the writer, except in the case of brief quotations embodied in critical reviews and certain other noncommercial uses permitted by copyright law.

This is a work of fiction. Names, characters, businesses, places, events and incidents are either the products of the author's imagination or used in a fictitious manner. Any resemblance to actual persons, living or dead, or actual events is purely coincidental.

Cover & Book Design by L.L. Frost

Printed in the United States of America.

First Printing, 2018

ALSO BY L. L. FROST

THE VEILS UNIVERSE

The (un)Lucky Succubus

First Serialized in Succubus Harem

Succubus Bargain

Succubus Studies

Succubus Mission

Succubus Hunted

Succubus Dreams

Succubus Trials

Succubus Undone

Succubus Reborn

Succubus Ascended

Demonic Messes (And Other Annoyances)

Drunk Girl *(novella)*

Doom Dog *(novella)*

The Cleaners

The Witchblood

The Fox God

Tally & Her Witches

MONSTERS AMONG US

Monsters Among Us: Hartford Cove

First Serialized in Hartford Cove

A Curse of Blood

Bathe Me In Red

A Feud to Bury

Harder

"**H**arder." I push up into Kellen's skillful touch.

He chuckles quietly. "Don't stop on your end."

My eyes flutter closed. "It feels so good when you press right—Ah."

His thumbs still on the arch of my foot. "Adie, this is supposed to be a mutual thing. If I'm doing all the rubbing, then you'll owe me something else in return."

"Fine." Grumbling, I pick his foot back up and prop it between my boobs to get back to work.

His foot is freaking enormous; my fingers barely overlap when I wrap my hands around the widest part. I wiggle for a better position on the floor where I lay in front of the chair Tobias usually sits in.

Both he and Emil were asleep long before I closed the bakery. When I arrived home, Kellen stood in the kitchen, reheating dinner, and one thing led to another. Somehow, I ended up on the floor with my feet in his lap while I reciprocated by rubbing his enormous platter feet.

I dig my thumbs into his hard heels. "I think two of my feet is worth one of yours."

"Then you should have bargained that before we started." His other foot lifts off the floor to nudge the side of my breast. "I'm getting both done tonight."

"So demanding." His toes slide toward my nipple, and I elbow it away. "I'm not giving you a boob massage."

Interest fills his voice. "Was that on the bargaining table?"

Considering, I abandon the foot rub to push my boobs together around his foot. It would be easier than using my hands. I eye his calluses. "Maybe if you exfoliate really, really well first."

"I haven't had a pedicure in years."

"I can tell." I pinch his heel hard. "Can you even feel this through all the calluses?"

"Yes, so don't stop. My feet are killing me."

When I wrap my hands back around his foot,

little sparklers dance down my palms before they burrow into my arms. They skate along my bones and dive into the core of energy that waits at my center.

"Did you have a long night at the Fulcrum?"

"The club wasn't too bad." He releases a deep sigh as he moves up to the ball of my foot. "Those dancers your cousin brought in are keeping the place lively."

When I first came to the human plane, it surprised me how many demons chose to work. Incubi and succubi tend to find rich humans and leech off them, accumulating fortunes that way so they never have to work. I thought my cousin Julian was the weird exception in running his HelloHell Delivery business until I ran into more and more demons who worked. My other roommates, Emil and Tobias, own and run K&B Financial, a local bank. It fits them, though. Men of power, amassing more power.

Life would get boring after a couple centuries if all they did was wander around aimlessly. Especially after they were told they were no longer allowed to destroy major civilizations.

Though, Kellen came dangerously close when he got caught up in a summer storm that came into the city. While it wouldn't have wrecked an entire civilization, it could have seriously damaged the city we live in and Kellen would have been stripped of his corporeal form, locked back on the demon plane.

My roommates are all demons of destruction and they need me, a half-functional succubus, to drain off their energy.

The static energy that Kellen releases nips against my fingers. While I'm skimming, it doesn't make much of a dent with this small amount of skin-to-skin contact. At least the summer storms finally left the area. Kellen needed daily draining while the storms were in town, constantly refueling him.

I slip my hands up his pant leg and press my bare forearms to the sides of his feet for more contact. The sparks turn into mini lightning bolts that dive into my body. In Kellen's grip, my toes flex with pleasure.

"Adie, you stopped rubbing," Kellen admonishes with a growl. "If you want to skim some other way, I'm open to suggestions, but I *will* be getting my foot rub tonight."

"I'm rubbing, I'm rubbing." I press a knuckle into the meat below his big toe, reconsidering the whole boob massage thing. That really would be easier.

"How's the bakery coming along? We barely see you at home lately."

His tone sounds light, but something sits below the surface. I glance up at him to find his lightning-kissed gaze focused on my feet. While all the guys are difficult to read, Kellen's usually the easiest. He's upfront with his desires, so why do I suddenly feel like I've failed him in some way?

Getting Boo's Boutique Bakery up and running keeps me there during the times the guys are off work, and while Kellen's club has him on a similar schedule, our paths rarely cross. He either arrives home before me and goes straight to bed, or I arrive home first and go straight to bed. Tonight is a rare opportunity for company. Although fatigue drags at both of us, it's unexpectedly nice to just hang out together like this.

His foot bounces in my grip, reminding me where my focus *should* be, and I drop my gaze. "It's going good. The imps are settling in nicely, though I think Kelly will leave once his contract is up. He's *really* interested in carpentry work." I peek up at Kellen again. "I was going to ask if Jax might give him some tips since he already knows about the imps?"

Kellen shifts to peer down at me. "Jax might be up for that. Do you want me to ask him?"

I bite my lips. "Is he really safe?"

As a general rule, humans aren't supposed to know about demons. There's a long history of slaughter on both sides that say it's a bad idea. But sometimes, humans find out anyway. Whether or not they keep their mouths shut determines whether they get to live, and we get to keep our corporeal forms on the human plane. I was surprised to discover Kellen revealed his secret to his human second in command at Fulcrum, Slater.

Then again, they live with my co-baker, Tally, who's a baku demon.

"None of them will give us away." His voice drops to an ominous purr. "Not if they want to stay where they're at right now."

I lift up onto my elbows, and his foot slips to the floor. "What's that mean?"

His hard gaze meets mine. "I own them."

Destruction demon.

A shiver rolls down my spine as I'm reminded once again that Kellen isn't always the playful, good-natured guy he presents himself to be. Gotta remember that. Kellen, Tobias, and Emil come from a time when demons were revered as gods, and the human plane was their playground.

His gaze becomes considering as he stares down at me, then slowly lifts my legs off his lap and sets them on the floor.

My pulse flutters with panic and excitement, and I lick my lips. "Are we done with foot rubs?"

"You're not really dedicated to it." He curls his fingers in invitation. "Isn't the floor hard on your back? Come up here."

"I..." Sitting up, I glance at the couch behind me. "The chair's kind of small for two. I can—"

"Adie, come up here." The quiet command makes my bones shake.

Serious Kellen isn't someone I'm used to dealing with, and it makes me nervous. My eyes skitter away from his. "I think I need to head to bed now."

His hand touches my cheek, little sparks snapping against my cheek. "Don't go. I need—" He swallows hard, and my gaze shoots back to his. "Just a little more?"

Unlike the others, who wait patiently for me to come to them, Kellen usually just gloms onto me when he needs to be drained. That he's asking now shoots alarm through me.

I scramble into his lap. "You should have just

said so from the beginning. Is there a storm nearby?"

"Yeah, a really big one." His hands slip under my shirt to skate static along my back. "I don't know if I can resist this one."

"Don't worry, I'll keep you on the ground." My thighs settle on either side of his, and I cup my hands around the back of his neck, my fingers threading through his fiery-red hair. "Just don't fight me this time, okay?"

"I can't promise that." His hands inch higher and circle my rib cage until his thumbs brush the sides of my breasts. "When the storms are strong, I want all the power." He leans forward to inhale over my skin. "You smell good, like there's a mini storm inside you, too."

Goosebumps rise on my bare arms. "Don't try to eat me."

"But you're so tempting." His lips brush along my throat, and I gasp in the taste of ozone and thunderstorms that hangs in the air.

It settles on the back of my tongue, a temptation to devour more, to latch onto Kellen and drain him to extinction. Does he feel the same when he touches me? My kind are born of passion and storms. Do I call to him the same way storms do?

My fingers curl in his hair, fisting his short locks as I tug his head back. His open lips beckon me closer, to the lightning and thunder, to the hurricanes and tsunamis that live inside him. He'll make me strong, strong enough to never fear another run in with my evil cousin Cassandra, strong enough to get back into Dreamland. And all it will take is everything he has.

His eyelids drop to veil his heated gaze. "Are you going to devour me, Adie?"

My muscles coil tight, ready to spring, but his expression whispers at me to be cautious. *Destruction demon. Destruction demon.* The reminder rattles through me, and my wings rustle against my spine, unsure if I should attack or flee.

My tongue darts out to skim my lips and take a quick taste of the ozone-laden air.

Despite the energy I already hold, hunger gnaws at my belly. I inch closer, dragging his breaths across my tongue, filling my lungs with the hint of his power. His hands add subtle pressure on my back to urge me on, and my wings razorblade against my spine in alarm. My thighs tense against his, ready to hyper-speed away.

As if he senses it, he grabs the back of my head and pulls me down, his lips slanting over mine.

Hands moving to his shoulders, my arms stiffen, ready to push him away. But then the taste of him hits my tongue, and I groan with pleasure. My arms loop around his neck to lock him in place as I dip into his mouth, lapping at the energy that waits for me. It trickles down my throat, crackling and jumping like pop rocks, to land in my belly. Heat suffuses my limbs and pools between my thighs.

My legs shift, trying to curl around his waist to better align my core over his hard cock, but the chair fights my efforts. I wiggle in frustration, momentarily distracted, and Kellen strikes. His tongue thrusts into my mouth, the thin stream of power reversing in an instant to flow back into him. I groan in surprised pleasure, then growl a warning.

My energy.

Eyes flicking open, I meet his hungry gaze as I catch the stream and yank it back. It becomes a struggle for dominance as we fight over the flow. Our bodies tense and strain against each other, and the leather of the chair creaks in warning. I grab the back of it for support, shifting for the more advantageous position over Kellen, and the support gives.

Kellen's mouth leaves mine as we fall back with surprised shouts, our upper bodies angling toward the floor. I sprawl across Kellen's chest, confused, but he barely hesitates before he reaches for me again, ready to continue.

From the right side of the fireplace, heavy footsteps pound down the stairs.

A moment later, a sleep-rumpled Tobias enters the room. His black gaze takes in the destruction of his favorite chair, and the white bleeds from his eyes. When the air becomes heavy with the weight of avalanches, I scramble into an upright position, still straddling Kellen.

I point at the storm demon. "It's his fault!"

From the other staircase, Emil appears with Tac peering over his head from a few steps above. "What's going on?"

I double point at Kellen and repeat. "It's his fault!"

Kellen folds his arms behind his head and grins. "Adie got too aggressive and broke the chair."

I whip around to glare down at him. "You were fighting the energy draw."

"Why were you doing an energy draw at four o'clock in the morning?" Tobias rumbles with the sound of rock slides. The house shivers in response.

My shoulders hunch in self-defense. "Because

there's a storm coming in. I needed to keep Kellen grounded."

"It's clear skies for the next week," Emil snaps with the bite of ice.

I stiffen, remembering now how thin the stream of energy was. My hands tense against Kellen's rock hard abs, my nails digging into his muscles. "Excuse me?"

"Learn to check the weather report." Emil turns and pushes at Tac. "I'm going back to bed."

"One of you owes me a new chair." Tobias's black gaze shifts between us. "It better be exactly like the one you broke."

His anger pulls back, the air becoming easier to breathe as he stomps back up to his room.

I glare down at Kellen. "You tricked me."

"I'm a demon." As he shrugs, his muscles ripple under me. "You should be less easy to trick."

"You're replacing the chair." I scramble off him, annoyed he's right. From now on, I'll make a point of checking the weather report every day.

"We can go half and half on it," he counters as he sits up.

I rise onto my toes. "You chose to sit there, you replace it."

His eyes narrow. "You technically broke it, you replace it."

"I'm broke!"

"Not my problem!"

"Shut up!" Emil yells from upstairs. "Some people are trying to sleep!"

My voice lowers to a whisper, "We can argue about it later. I'm going to bed."

When I spin away, Kellen catches my wrist. "Hey, what about rubbing my feet?"

Mouth popping open in shock, I stare at him. "Are you serious?"

His gaze remains steady. "We already bargained for it."

Wings rustling against my spine with irritation, I plop back on the floor, lie down, and thrust my feet into his lap. "Fine, but I'm not going to like it."

His heels plant themselves under by boobs, toes wiggling for attention. "Don't worry, I'll enjoy this enough for the both of us."

Not an Offering

When my alarm goes off the next morning, I thrust an arm out of my pillow burrow, grab the damn thing from the headboard, and chuck it across the room. It lands with a loud crash, and the high-pitched beep cuts off. Curling more snuggly around my purple sequin pillow, I close my eyes once more.

The rush of water fills the pipes as, downstairs, Emil gets into the shower.

I bolt upright, pillows bouncing to the floor, and push the hair from my face. It's morning; I have a plan. Kellen's words from last night stuck with me, and I realized I actually miss seeing my frequently prickly roommates.

Scrambling out of bed, I stumble downstairs to the kitchen. At the stove, I turn on the kettle to heat water, turn on the stove to preheat, then hyper-speed around the kitchen to gather supplies: flour, sugar, eggs, milk, butter, vanilla, oranges. Emil likes sweets, but Tobias prefers savory.

Plopping a mixing bowl onto my new kitchen scale, I measure out the ingredients for sunshine muffins. Close to a cupcake, but with less sugar. I've been working on the new flavor for the bakery and think I've nailed the right balance of citrus and vanilla to make them perfect. I whisk the flour and leaveners to aerate the mix before I set it aside. In a new bowl, I whip the butter and sugar together until it turns a beautiful, pale yellow, then add the eggs one at a time.

The motions fill me with happiness, and I hum as the mixture comes together, the flakes of orange zest giving the batter a delightful, speckled appearance. Sweet and tart fill the air, and my wings rustle and slip free from my back to flutter gently.

I first learned to cook as a self-defense mechanism. Landon, my mentor, only orders delivery, and I couldn't live off of fried chicken and biscuits. Teaching myself was difficult, especially since he turned his kitchen into a butterfly garden, but I managed. And I discovered I truly love the process of combining plain ingredients to create mouth-watering cakes. Like the alchemy of old, the transformation entrances me. The exchange of one thing for another.

I scoop the batter evenly into muffin cups and pop them into the oven just as the kettle begins its first, quiet whistle.

Zooming around the kitchen, I pick out a hot chocolate for Emil and a tea for Tobias to compliment the orange flavored muffins and prep their to-go cups. At the drawer of straws, I spot a cheery yellow one and snap it up to pop into Emil's cup to give the ice demon as much distance from his hot beverage as possible. When he has to put his mouth directly on a cup, it freezes over instantly. Poor guy.

Everything else ready, I clean up my small mess and get the bowls and utensils put away. Emil hates a messy kitchen, and this morning is about spreading happiness.

With only a few minute left, I bounce on my toes, gaze fixed on the oven. The warm glow invites me to come closer, to peer through the clear glass doors at the soft domes that peek over the top of the muffin tin.

Perfect. So perfect.

That can be said about a lot of things right now in my life. While I haven't made it back into

Dreamland, I now know how to; it will just take time. And in the interim, I have my business, and I live in a house with an amazing kitchen.

My chest fills with warmth as I pet the handles on the french doors of the oven. "Who's a beautiful oven? You are. Yes, you are."

"What are you doing?" Tobias drawls.

I spring to my feet, wings snapping back into hiding. "Nothing?"

"You were talking to the oven again, weren't you?"

My hands fold behind my back. "Nope!"

His thick eyebrow arches. "You *know* that's a standard, human made oven right? There's no ignus demon?"

My eyes narrow. "Of course I do."

"So cooing at it won't make it cook better."

"I'm *baking*, not *cooking*." Irritation makes my fingers tighten on themselves. "And I'm not stupid."

Emil walks into the kitchen, his nose lifted into the air. "What smells so good?"

My good mood comes rushing back, and I skip over to him and plant a kiss on his chilly cheek. "Good morning!"

He glances at me from the corner of his eye, his

gaze suspicious. "Good morning, Adie. What has you up at this hour?"

"I haven't seen you guys much lately." The timer goes off, and I bounce back to the oven, pulling the muffins out.

Beautiful golden brown on top with high domes and a light crust. Eyes closed, I inhale the mouth-watering aroma. My wings slip free once more, the feathers spreading into a delighted stretch.

Perfect.

"I wish she'd look at us like that," Tobias mutters.

My eyes snap open, and I glance at him. "Like what?"

He gestures, his hands going wide to encompass my wings, which instantly snap back into hiding. "Like you can't wait to dig in."

My lips purse. "Maybe if you covered yourself in chocolate sauce, I'd give it a go."

His eyes take on a considering glint. "That can be arranged."

My tongue darts out to taste the ozone on the air as the two destruction demons come closer. Emil's hand lifts to his tie, as if to loosen it. "It's a bit messy for my taste, but if that's what you're into..."

"I'm not!" I throw the muffin tin onto the counter and scuttle away from them.

Tobias tracks my progress like a hunter spotting prey. "Are you sure?"

"Yes!" My wings rustle against my spine with interest, and heat floods my cheeks. In all my years in Dreamland, before I came to the human plane, I never fed from someone with a food kink. "Mostly sure!"

Emil's gaze shifts from me to the tray of muffins, then to his blue to-go cup with the yellow straw sticking out of it. "Did you wake up to make us breakfast?"

Now, I feel kind of foolish for doing it, but I stiffen my spine. "Yes, yes I did."

"Hmm." He uses one finger to drag the hot pan across the island. "I accept this method of courtship."

"Wha...?" My mouth drops open in surprise.

"It's passable," Tobias agrees as he plucks one of the muffins out and brings it to his nose. "I accept this offering."

My hands fly to my hips. "This is *not* an offering."

"It won't act as replacement for my chair,

though." His glare presses down on me. "This is not equal in value."

"I never said it was!" I point at them. "And this is *not* an offering! This is a *good morning fellow roommates who I haven't spent much time with lately.*"

"Bed-tousled hair, sexy lingerie"—Tobias's gaze sweeps over me—"you're definitely trying to entice us."

I glance down at my gray yoga pants that hang on my hips and my loose, white tank top. Not sexy at all. "Tobias, are you feeling okay? Maybe you should go lie back down?"

Emil's head tilts, attention fixed on my body. "It's like playing peek-a-boo. This is a new take on naked apron play, right?"

"What are you guys talking about?" I crane my neck, trying to see what they do. "Did one of my boobs pop out or something?"

"Don't ruin the fun," Tobias murmurs and takes a large bite of his muffin.

I stretch the ribbed material over my breasts, and the thick material hides my nipples. My wings razorblade with irritation. "What are you guys talking about?"

In answer, Emil stuffs an entire muffin into his mouth.

"I like this recipe." Tobias's attention shifts to the half-eaten muffin in his hand. "It's not too sweet."

My wings pop out of my back as joy shoots through me. "You really like it?"

Both men grin, and my wings snap back into hiding. Their smiles disappear with deep sighs of disappointment.

I cover my bare shoulders. "Stop looking at them!"

"You should let them out more often," Tobias rumbles, and Emil nods in agreement. "It can't be comfortable to keep them trapped all the time."

"We're not discussing my wings!" I'd rather prance around naked then have my wings out for them to stare at.

Emil selects another muffin. "They're cute."

Fire fills my cheeks. "Shut up."

"I want to touch them." Tobias's hands open as if he imagines the feathers in his fingers. "Especially the ones next to your spine."

"No!" My wings try to slip free, and I force them to stay hidden. "No touching the wings."

"It will feel good," Tobias purrs, the whites bleeding from his eyes.

The air turns heavy with his desire, and my tongue darts out to taste the power that seeps from him. Uncertain, I rise onto my tiptoes to make myself bigger. "Not happening."

His black gaze holds me transfixed. "You don't sound too certain about that."

A cold hand touches my arm, and I shriek with fright. Spinning, I find Emil at my side. When did he move?

Undeterred by my outburst, he leans in and presses a cold kiss against my cheek. "Thank you for breakfast, Adie. It was delightful."

Attention darting back to Tobias to make sure he hasn't come closer, I reach out to give Emil's hand a quick squeeze. Ice creeps under my skin to slide along my bones. "You're welcome."

He lifts our linked hands to kiss my knuckles, his icy-blue eyes catching mine. "Next time you have a free night, will you make pasta and cannoli?"

Embarrassed warmth floods through me to fight back his winter chill. My pulse flutters at the reminder of our psuedo-date from a couple weeks ago. Was this him flirting with me again? "Yeah, I can do that."

"I like cannoli, too." Tobias presses against my other side, and I flinch at the volcanic heat that radiates from his body. "Would you be willing to share?'

Emil's gaze flickers to him. "I'll take the request under consideration."

"Umm, guys"—I wiggle between them, cold on one side, hot on the other—"I can make enough for everyone."

They stare at each other over the top of my head, some power battle playing out, and I realize maybe they're not actually talking about Italian desserts.

Heart racing, I leap away from them. "Okay, have a good day at work! I'm going back to bed!"

"You can cuddle up with Tac if you like," Emil calls after me as I fast walk for the open archway that leads to escape. "I don't mind."

"No thanks, I'm good!" I call over my shoulder and quicken my pace into an almost run.

No way I can roll up in sheets that smell like Emil, that hold the power of glaciers, and get any more sleep. My thundering heart already makes my limbs shaky.

Tobias's voice reaches me as I place my foot on the bottom stair. "Feel free to join us anytime. Your offerings are appreciated."

"Not an offering!" I yell back and run for the dubious safety of my bedroom.

When I wake up five hours later, I feel like total crap. It took forever to force myself back to sleep, then my dreams were plagued with knights in shiny armor, battling giant cat monsters. When I crawl out of my nest of pillows, I'm not surprised to find Tac sprawled across the lower two thirds of my bed. Despite his closed eyes, his tufted tail swishes back and forth off the side of the bed.

Since I've been trying to read his desires to build on my succubus powers, a constant hunger for metal and leather clad humans persistently fills my mind. I press my palms between his eyes and give him a firm rub. "I'm sorry you can't eat knights anymore, big guy."

His chainsaw purr shakes the bed as saucer sized green eyes slit open to stare at me. He inches forward on his belly until his wedge-shaped head nudges against my stomach, his ears swiveling for attention.

Laughing, I rub the edges of one with both hands. "Do you think the guys saved you any sunshine muffins?"

His rumble increases to rattle my bones.

"If they didn't, I'll make you a fresh batch. Some

for Kellen, too." I lean down to rest my cheek between his ears. "Can't show any favoritism in this house, right?"

He snuffles, his breath hot through my tank top.

"Okay, fine," I whisper. "You're my favorite, but don't tell the others."

He releases a contented sigh, and I straighten to pet his other ear. The cat monster really is one of the best parts of living here. Even if he only sneaks into my room in the morning after Emil leaves for work. When I tried to entice him to sleep with me as soon as I got home from work, he rustled his bat like wings at me and attached himself to the ice demon's side. Guess I know who *his* favorite in the house is. But my treats will win him over eventually.

I grab his fluffy jowls and lift his head. "Yes, they will. Just you wait."

His nostrils flutter, and moist air blows the hair back from my face.

I grin. "You're just playing hard to get, aren't you?"

In answer, his lips pull back to reveal dagger-sized canines in a grin of his own.

"Okay, enough snuggling. Time to get ready for work." I pat his head. "Thanks for making me feel less crappy, big guy. You're a real energy boost."

While I don't skim energy off Tac, his fluffy goodness really does brighten my mood. He rolls onto his back, stomach in the air.

I shake a finger at him. "No, you will *not* keep me in bed."

His paws tuck against his chest, his liquid gaze fixed on me.

"Okay, fine." I sprawl across his soft belly. "Who can resist this?"

An hour later, I finally make it back downstairs, showered, dressed, and ready to head into the bakery.

When I walk into the kitchen, I jump with surprise to find Kellen once again seated at the counter. I check the clock to make sure Tac didn't keep me enamored longer than I thought, but the hour hand says Kellen should still be sleeping.

The storm demon glances up from his cup of coffee, his lightning eyes less bright. "You're up early."

"So are you." I circle to the fridge and pull out an iced tea. "I'm on baking duty today."

"I have a meeting with a new liquor guy." We share a smile before Kellen lifts a large, container from the counter. "Did you make these?"

I spot my sunshine muffins through the hazy plastic. "Yep, I made breakfast for everyone."

"You're a goddess." He cracks the lid open and pulls one out. "I don't have time to stop at the donut shop on the way in today."

Tac comes lumbering into the kitchen and settles at Kellen's side, his eyes fixed on the muffins. I lean over to grab one and toss it into his waiting maw.

Kellen grunts. "Don't waste these on Tac."

"He's part of the household, too. Everyone gets treated equally." I toss another into the cat monster's mouth. "This is called sharing."

"That must be one of those newfangled words you youngsters are using these days." Kellen grabs the container and pulls it out of my reach. "The rest are mine."

"Hey, I haven't had any either." I lean into his side, reaching for the container.

His arm loops around my shoulders, pressing me close while keeping me away from my goal. "If you wanted to continue to snuggle, you could have just come to bed with me last night."

I dig hard fingers into his ribs. "I won't be lured so easy."

"So I've noticed." He captures my fingers. "Come to the club tonight."

I frown at him. "I won't be done at the bakery until after you close."

He lifts feathery golden eyebrows. "Don't you think it's time you trust Tally to close on her own?"

"Well..." I nibble on my lower lip.

"You've shadowed her for weeks now. I think she can handle it," he cajoles.

Suspicious, I lean harder against his side until he tilts off center on his stool. "Why do you want me to come?"

"You haven't come to dance since before you moved in." He shifts until both arms circle my waist, his face close. "Come dance with me."

Flustered by the request, my eyes dart away from his. "Won't you be busy?"

"I'll make time." He nuzzles my cheek and sparkles dance along my skin.

My heartbeat spikes. "Like, a..." I lick my lips and taste coppery lightning. My voice comes out thready. "Like a date?"

He leans back to stare down at me, his face serious. "Yes, Adie, like a date."

My eyes widen in wonder. "You want to date me?"

"You seem enamored of the way humans do things, so yes, I'd like to *date* you." Lightning skitters across his pupils, and his voice vibrates with the hint of thunder. "It's only fair, since Emil already took you on one, right? Everything equal?"

I taste the air again, committing the flavor of Kellen's jealousy to memory. Hesitant, I offer. "We could go shopping sometime this week, too. To replace Tobias's chair?"

Kellen grins. "I know just the places to look."

Happy, my wings try to slip free, but I keep them locked in place. This is going to become a bad habit around these guys. "I'll text you when I'm on my way over tonight, if that sounds good to you?"

He releases me. "I look forward to it."

Darting out a hand, I nab the last sunshine muffin and run for the door. I have preparations to make.

Girl Time

I pull my old sedan up in front of the GPS's final destination and double-check the text with Tally's address. They match. The dilapidated mansion Tally lives in comes as a shock. I always pictured her in a large apartment like what I used to live in or maybe a small house tucked into the residential part of town.

Instead, I find myself parked in the cracked driveway of a narrow three story house with small balconies on the second and third level that overlook the single car width street. Yellowed grass covers the small, open patches on either side of the driveway, and a cobblestone walkway leads to a sagging porch.

Someone tried to give the old thing a facelift by painting it a light tan, but their efforts go to waste as it peels in places to reveal the black beneath. At random intervals, lights flicker in the upper windows, like the circuits don't quite connect right.

Adding to that the twisted maze of alleys it took to reach the house, and Tally's home is one unwelcoming residence.

I push my car door open, careful not to knock against the black sedan that sits on the left side of the driveway, closer to the porch. I recognize it as the one the guys drive when they bring Tally to work. It looks too nice in front of this house. Out of place with its polished hubcaps and sparkling windows that show a well-cared for leather interior. If they can afford a nice car, why not a nicer place to live? Somewhere that looks less haunted.

Hugging my elbows, I eye the overhang for signs it's ready to come crashing down as I creep up onto the porch. When it appears I'm out of imminent danger, I glance to the front door and freeze.

The ugliest lion's head knocker I've ever seen stares back at me, red jeweled eyes flickering despite the deep shadows of the porch. Sharp fangs curl around the metal ring, the lips lifted in a snarl that dares me to come closer.

Maybe I should just text Tally that I'm here...

Before I can retreat, the door flies open, and Tally fills the entrance, pink hair vibrating with excitement. "Adie! I'm so happy you called!"

A surprised grunt escapes me as the baku demon throws her arms around me and gives me a tight hug. Her unique scent of clay tickles at my nose and makes me want to sneeze.

Over her head, I spot a polished marble foyer, with a curved staircase that leads up to a second floor walkway. A crystal chandelier throws rainbows of colors around the room and makes it impossible to see the framed artwork on the walls from the porch.

Tally releases me and steps back, her hands clasped in front of her chest. "I've never had a girls' day before. This will be so much fun!"

"Well, we don't have a lot of time before we need to be at the bakery..." Flustered, I tug on the braid of white hair that hangs over my shoulder. I've never had a girls' day either, but TV tells me they're supposed to involve lunch and a trip to a salon, too. "I just want to get one new outfit for tonight."

Her mahogany eyes brighten. "For a special occasion?"

"Well..." Blood warms my cheeks. "Maybe a date with Kellen." When she begins to bounce with excitement, I rush to add, "But it's only at his club. Nothing special."

"Don't downplay it! This is exciting!" She reaches back into the house and comes back with a large, pink purse that she slings over one shoulder. "We will find you the best outfit!"

I duck my head with embarrassment. Is this really what it's like to have a female friend? It fills me with bubbles of happiness. "Thank you for coming with me."

"Of course!" She turns to the open door and raises her voice. "I will be leaving now!"

An auburn head pops out from around the staircase, a pair of wire-rimmed glasses perched on his nose. A moment later, Xander walks into the foyer.

He wears sweatpants and a rumpled t-shirt, but his brown eyes study us with alertness as he pulls off his glasses. "Tally, if you wait, I'll go with you. I'm almost at a stopping place on my project."

Tally's hands move to her hips. "If you came, it would not be a *girls'* day."

"If you're *sure* you'll be okay." Frowning with

uncertainty, he tugs on a necklace that hangs around his neck.

The clay piece releases the faint smell of demonic ozone. Each of the guys wears one, but I've never asked Tally what it's about. I suspect it has something to do with how a baku demon got out of Dreamland, but the less I know, the better. If they're breaking some demonic law, I can't be forced to report on something I don't know.

"Adie will be with me." She lays a cool hand on my arm. "She is strong enough to crush anyone who bothers me."

Xander eyes me with doubt, and I puff out my chest. "I can take care of Tally. No problem."

For a brief moment, his eyes drop to my boobs. They're impressive and receive a lot of attention—I'm a succubus after all—but disinterest fills his gaze before it moves back to Tally and softens. "You have your phone."

She pats her bag. "Yes."

"You have your backup phone?"

She pats the pocket on her jeans with a sigh. "Yes."

"You have cash in case your cards don't work?"

Her cheeks puff out with irritation. *"Xander."*

His eyes narrow. "You ate the dreams of those self-defense instructors."

Face turning bright pink, she grabs my arm and tugs me toward the porch stairs. "We are leaving now!"

"Did you grab a bottle of water?" he calls as he hovers in the doorway.

Her steps slow for a second, and she eyes her enormous purse with uncertainty. I lean close to whisper in her ear. "We can buy some on the way."

"I will be fine, Xander!" she yells without looking back. "Return to your work."

"I'll be by the bakery later!"

She peeks back with a scowl. "You do not need to come!"

"*Don't*, Tally! Use contractions!"

Her shoulders hunch. "He is such a *mother* sometimes." In the next instant, she brightens as she releases me to skip around to the passenger side door of my car. "Where will we be shopping?"

"I figured the mall." I glance back at the house. Xander now hovers at the porch rail, his hand on his necklace. With a wave, I climb into my car and reach across the seat to unlock Tally's side. As she slides in, I say, "Your roommates. They sure do care about you a lot."

"Yes, but it is a lot of..." Her pink brows furrow. "Testosterone? They worry too much and tend to think they know best."

Starting the car, I let out a laugh. "Yeah, guys are like that, no matter their species."

She twists in her seat. "So, tell me. How did Kellen ask you on your date?"

∽

"Adie, Adie, you must get this one. It is *beautiful*." Tally holds the floral print dress up under her chin. With her pink hair, the large, violet flowers on a gray background make her look like someone who belongs at a candy store. Or selling cupcakes.

When she extends one of the long sleeves to reveal lace at the cuffs, I cough to suppress my laugh. "I think that would be lovely on you, but I'm looking for something that shows more skin."

With a frown, Tally pokes her leg out from under the knee length hem. "But the skirt flounces so nicely."

"I bet Xander would like to see you in that."

Contemplative, she swishes the dress back and forth. "Do you think so?"

I really have no idea. Her men tend to keep to themselves. But I'm sure they'd appreciate her dressing up for them regardless. Smiling, I tell her, "You should try it on."

She checks the price tag and nibbles on her plump, bottom lip. "I *do* have the plastic cards."

Leaving her to decide, I turn back to the rack of dresses in front of me. In the middle of summer, light, strappy dresses seem to be in demand. But the pastel colors will look out of place at a club at night.

I circle around the rack, and my eyes catch on a steel gray dress with a swirly, fractal pattern that reminds me of clouds. When I lift it from the rack and hold it up, it stops at mid-thigh with a circular skirt that will flare out when I spin. I imagine Kellen's expression if he sees me in something that so closely resembles his sigil and start to put it back, unsure I want to brand myself as his on our first date.

"Oh, Adie, that's *perfect*," Tally gushes as she leans against my side. "And it will leave so much exposed."

"I think I'll keep looking." But my fingers tighten on the hanger.

"Nonsense!" Tally tugs the dress from my hands. "Let's go find a changing room!"

Before she gets too far, I snag a couple other options from the rack and hurry after her.

I catch up to her just as she reaches the lady at the security counter and announces, "We would like the large dressing room, please!"

The bored employee nods. "How many items?"

Tally holds the two dresses in her hands up. "Two!"

"Five, actually." I show my hangers, too, then glance at Tally with a lifted brow. "You don't want your own room?"

"How will I give you my opinion if we're in separate rooms?"

"Okay." I shrug, not worried about her seeing me naked and kind of curious to see what she's hiding.

She doesn't smell like a demon, she's cooler to the touch than most humans, and there's that odd clay smell that clings to her. Maybe she's some kind of golem? Her guy, Reese, is fae touched, maybe him and his brother constructed her a body to inhabit? Images of smooth dolls pop into my head. Maybe I have their relationship all wrong?

We follow the security lady to the end of the dressing rooms, where she unlocks a door that's wider than the rest. When she pushes it open, a narrow bench fills the back wall with metal handrails secured to the walls on either side, bisecting the mirrors.

Tally veers to the left to hang up my dress, then bounces across the room to the right hand wall where she hangs up her selection.

"Let me know if you need anything," the lady says, already turning to walk back to her post.

"Thank you!" I call after her.

When I turn back, Tally slipped her shirt off already and is working on her pants. Quickly, I shut the door before anyone else walks by.

I go to my side of the room and turn my back to give Tally a semblance of privacy as I undress and put on the first of the dresses, a white sundress with yellow sunflowers. My boobs stretch the low top to the point where I think they might pop out on the dance floor. Kellen probably wouldn't care, but human laws are picky about things like public exposure.

"I don't like that one at all," Tally chimes in from behind me.

I turn to find her still in her undergarments, and it surprises me to discover she wears conservative cotton underwear and a sports bra. Not revealing at all. So much for my curiosity.

She eyes my dress with distaste and shakes her head. "Just try on the gray one. You know that's the one you really want."

I tug on the front of the dress to hike it a little higher. "Yeah, I know. I'm just...worried about it."

"How come?" She pulls her own dress over her head, and I smile. She really does look like some kind of confection. I should make a cupcake based on her. Strawberries and cream, with sprinkles. She tilts her head. "Adie?"

Shaking myself, I turn to pull off the white dress and pick up the steel gray one. My fingers run over the white fractals. "This is my first date with Kellen, and this dress might give him the wrong impression."

"How so?" She comes to stand at my side. "It's only a dress."

I lift the skirt. "Do you think these look like storm clouds?"

She bends closer, her expression serious. "I believe they look like swirly lines."

"Really?" At her firm nod, my shoulders sag with relief, and I pull the dress over my head.

"That's a relief. I didn't want Kellen to think I was purposefully wearing his symbols."

"Would it matter that much?" She tugs on the skirt, making it sway. "It is good to let your men know of your interest."

"Kellen can be a little...competitive with his interest." I adjust the spaghetti straps. "I don't want him to take this as a white flag of surrender."

"If he crosses the line, you simply need to stop him." She squeezes my bicep. "You are strong."

A laugh escapes me. "I appreciate your confidence, but he's pretty strong, too."

"You can crush him. No problem." She points at me. "You are a devourer. You can turn him to dust."

I cringe at the term. While succubi and baku both devour parts of humans, most baku can't kill them simply by eating their dreams. And succubi are known to eat the lesser baku demons in Dreamland when they become too powerful.

Through the mirror, I catch her gaze. "How come you weren't afraid of me when we met?"

Her head tilts in consideration before she admits, "I stalked you in Dreamland."

I whip around to stare down at her. "You did what now?"

Red stains her cheeks. "Your cousins talk about

you. Adeline Boo Pond, raised by the fearsome Landregath the Great Devourer, who can't re-enter Dreamland. You're a bit of a celebrity to my kind."

My lips twist. "That makes me sound like a daytime soap opera."

"Yes." Her simple, uncensored response takes some of the sting out of the revelation. "Many are curious how things will play out for you. Moving in with the Demons of Destruction was an interesting plot twist."

My eyes dart around the changing room, and I lower my voice. "Are we being watched right now?"

"Always." Her eyes flick back to the mirror, and her nose wrinkles. "I'm a celebrity, too. The baku who lives on the human plane." Her voice rises. "I've come to find it's very *intrusive*."

I cross my arms over my chest. "I'm not sure how I feel about this."

"At least, you can't see them in the shadows." Her gaze drops to the bench where a large swath of shadow waits at the back. "Go home, Aren."

A moment of silence passes before she scowls. "No, I don't want to see you at the bakery later."

Crouching, I peer into the shadows but only see the darker beige wall.

Tally huffs out an annoyed breath. "Aren says to tell you he is excited for your date tonight."

"Thank you?"

"He also says to tell you to wear different underwear tonight." Her hands turn into tiny fists she plants on her hips. "No, I will not be relaying your suggestions."

"Okay, this is weird, even for me." I spool out some of the energy that rolls in my belly and push it outward in a bubble shaped wave.

While I can't see Aren, I feel his presence at the edge of my energy, a dark mist I sweep out through the wall. Sweat breaks out over my brow, but the effort is worth it when Tally grins at me.

She rubs the goosebumps from her arms. "Most excellent."

"I can't maintain it indefinitely, but at least we can have some privacy for now." Already, the energy in my belly feels lower, the ball shrinking to leave hunger behind.

It gives me new, scary respect for Landon. He pushed out enough energy to force cousin Cassandra back. Not something I could do. While my energy wall swept Aren out of the room, it didn't even budge Tally in her physical form.

Tally flips the hem of the third dress with

disinterest. "Shall you try on the other dress while we are alone?"

"No, I think I'll get this one." I brush a hand over the swirls. "As long as you *really* don't think they look like storm clouds."

Her head bobs, expression serious. "They *really* don't."

(Un)Perfect

I crouch in front of the line of shadow between the ovens and wall. "I appreciate all of your help, but I really need you to wear a hairnet in the kitchen." I touch the one that covers my tight bun, then hold out the fresh one in my hand. "It's a human law we must obey."

The domovoi's gray eyebrows bristle.

"See, it just goes on like this." Slowly, so I don't scare him, I stretch out the elastic and slip it over his pointed ears, cover his furry head, and tuck it under his large lobes. With a little fussing, I get his eyebrows covered. His bright, yellow owl eyes blink at me, first the right, then the left, and his bulbous nose twitches.

"Oh, you look very fashionable," Tally gushes from over my shoulder. "So handsome."

He blinks faster, the fur on his head fluffing up under the net with pride.

"Now, you're an official crew member." I place my hands on my knees, ready to stand.

Sloth slow, one chubby-fingered hand reaches out to touch my knee, and I freeze. The domovoi has never touched me directly nor spoken. But when we come in every morning, the counters glisten, and Torch's food bowl always has a fresh layer of pellets. This morning, when I arrived to the fresh smell of cupcakes baking, I knew it was time to talk about health codes.

Now, I lean closer to the domovoi. "Yes?"

He pats his chest. "Vova."

Tally's excitement fills the air, a mirror of mine, but I keep my expression respectful. "It's a pleasure to know your name, Vova."

As if that's as much as the little kitchen demon can manage for the day, he slides back into the shadows and vanishes.

"This is good." Tally shakes my shoulders. "Really, really good!"

I nod with amazement as I stand. I never thought we'd gain the domovoi's trust so fast. It usually takes years of offerings to get to the name stage. Turning, I smile at the pink-haired demon who quickly became my first female friend on this plane. "Things are really looking up."

"We have another request for a party." Tally claps. "I put the information on your desk."

"Thank you." I turn to stare at the bustling kitchen.

Imps walk around with confidence, each focused on their own task. Even the unformed one seems to be coming out of its shell, scurrying around under the elbows of its brethren to fetch clean plates. Trays of cupcakes cool on the kitchen carts in preparation for decorations, while, through the passthrough, I spot a long line of customers at the counter. Happy customers fill almost every table in the front of the shop.

Boo's Boutique Bakery flourished faster than I predicted when I first walked into K&B Financial with my business proposition. If this were a human owned and financed business, I'd be breaking even after business expenses. But since Emil demands non-monetary compensation from the demons he offers loans to, I'm actually making a tidy profit right now. Enough that, if I needed to move out of the guys' house, I'd be able to cover my rent once more.

My chest tightens with panic at that idea, and I

push it away. There's no reason the guys would kick me out right now. Kellen and Emil even want to *date* me.

My toes curl at thought. I've never *dated* anyone before, and I look forward to the experience.

Whatever bad luck plagued me seems to have run its course.

Everything's looking up in the life of Adeline Boo Pond.

Trepidation sings in my blood, and I search the crowded front for what brought on the sudden shift in mood.

"Adie?" Tally touches my elbow. "You okay?"

Awareness vibrates against my bones. Something wicked entered my shop. But when I scan the customers, all the humans look happy. My sigil remains quiet on the cupcake display glass, and a quick check on the shadow line shows Vova still in hiding. Whatever brought on this feeling isn't demonic or intending the shop harm.

I tear my attention from the front to meet Tally's worried, mahogany gaze. "Do you feel something off?"

She shakes her head. "No, but I can't sense emotions like you can."

Worried, I pull the hairnet off my head. "I'm

going to call the imps back here and man the register for a bit."

Her fingers fold together over her chest. "Do you want me to help?"

"Keep an eye on the back door and make sure Torch stays small."

Eyes wide, she nods her agreement.

Determined, I march through the swinging door. Time to see if my practice in mind reading paid off.

∼

After two hours up front, my head pounds, and strain makes my eyes hurt. Humans are a lot harder than Tac. They bury their desires deeper, hiding from even themselves. The immediate ones, like sex and hunger, come with little flashes of pictures when I brush against their bare skin while taking money or handing out desserts. But the darker desires stay out of reach, shadows that dance just outside my ability to grasp.

As the next human steps up to the counter, I catch her gaze and put a little whammy behind it. Not enough to beguile her, but enough to make her more susceptible. Her happy expression fades away, her mouth slackening.

My pain in my head increases as I try to guess which flavor cupcake she desires. That should be easy enough. "What can I get for you today?"

The color yellow forms in my mind. Sunflower maybe?

She licks her lips. "I want to be banged by construction workers."

Hard hats. Damn it!

When I let the whammy go, she snaps back to reality, embarrassed as she glances around in confusion. "Umm, sorry, what did you ask?"

I smile to ease her tension. Nothing weird here. Just your friendly neighborhood bakery. "What flavor cupcake would you like today?"

"Umm, the blue rose?" Her eyes flick to the customer behind her, and her shoulders sag with relief to find the mother preoccupied with her toddler. "Is that one chocolate?"

"Yes, it is!" I punch the order into the system. "Will that be for here or to go?"

She twists to check the seating options and blushes when her focus lands on the trio of construction workers across the street. "For here, please, with an iced coffee?"

"I'll have that right up for you!" I take her

money before moving to the espresso machine to get her coffee going.

Not having one of the imps up here slows down the ordering process, but so far, the mood remains light and happy.

At around six, the sense of looming danger dissipates.

While I tried to keep track of the customers who lingered at the tables, when I scan them once more, I can't spot any specific one now missing that could have been the cause of my concern.

I'm hesitant to bring the imps back out, though. They're mine to keep safe until cousin Julian sends his right hand man to fetch them back to their office. A lull in customers gives me a moment to catch my breath, and I pull out my phone. I should text Kellen and let him know I'm not coming tonight.

My stomach twists into a sour knot. I really wanted to go on my date with Kellen. I haven't been dancing in a while, not since I illegally skimmed energy from Fulcrum before I met the guys, and I want to immerse myself in a sea of humans with a hunger that gnaws at my bones. It's not even about feeding on them. The skin-on-skin contact brings with it a pleasure all of its own that I crave.

Tally pushes through the swinging door, a fresh

tray of lemon sunflower cupcakes held in front of her. She smiles as she scoots around me to the display case. "Don't you need to get ready soon?"

I fiddle with my phone. "I was about to cancel."

She pauses in the motion of swapping out the empty tray for the new one. "Why would you do that?"

"It feels like I should stay here." I glance around the shop, now half empty as the afternoon customers head home for dinner. The next rush will come around eight when the night crowd loads up on sugar before hitting the town.

Tally tucks the empty tray under her arm and turns to appraise me. "Are you sure you're not just nervous?"

Surprised, I take my eyes off an elderly couple to focus on her. "Why would I be nervous?"

"Well, you said it's a *date*." Her feathery pink eyebrows pinch together. "How many of those have you been on?"

"One, with Emil." I shrug. "But it's just dancing at Kellen's club. Nothing I can't handle."

"It's dancing with intention." Hidden by the countertop, she shakes her hips suggestively. "He's courting you."

I glance down at the phone, not wanting to miss tonight. "Yes, he is."

Tally squeezes my arm. "Go change. Everything will be fine here. And the club isn't that far away if you want to pop back in to check on us later."

"I suppose." Sliding the phone back into my pocket, I glance back over the shop. "Are you sure this isn't too long of a shift for you?"

"I'll take a break with Xander during the next lull." She waves at the corner table, which I've officially dubbed Tally's table.

Xander sits with his back to the wall, a laptop in front of him. Every so often, he wanders up to the counter to order a coffee or a snack from the case; although I catch him sneaking apple slices from his satchel, too. I've told her men they're not obligated to buy from the shop every day, but they continue to persist.

"Okay, I'm going." Nodding to give myself encouragement, I march back to the kitchen area and release Kelly and Iris to man the front once more. At the ovens, Vova crouches next to Torch's hatch, his fuzzy head still covered by a hairnet. Torch's door sits open, and the two seem to be conversing, if the flickers of yellow, blue, and white coming from the oven are any indication. None of the ovens look to be in use at the moment, so I leave them to it and head to the pantry/break room where the dress I purchased earlier hangs from the back of the door.

Quickly, I strip out of my uniform and into the dress, then unwind my bun. After being twisted up all day, my hair falls around my shoulders with gentle waves, the pale blue tips brighter against the steel gray of the dress. I take a moment to fuss with the hem, making sure it bells out properly when I spin. The soft material settles back at mid-thigh, a light caress against my skin that promises more to come.

After expending energy all day, it will be hard not to feed on the emotions that fill Kellen's club, but with the storm demon at my side, I'll be able to resist. His energy offers far more enticement than the emotions of humans.

Excitement shivers through my bones. Tonight is a new beginning for us. Possibly even a romantic connection.

I step back into my neon blue clogs, spin one more time, and open the pantry door.

As I step through, energy prickles along my skin, and the hallway of the bakery disappears to be replaced by a long corridor of doors with frosted glass windows. Behind me, the door back to the bakery slams and locks.

On her bright red scooter, the Librarian waits, her talons clicking as she grips her handlebars. "Keep up, girl, we have much to discuss."

And with that, she zooms away.

Perfect.

The Assignment

"Ummm, excuse me!" I yell as I sprint after the Librarian.

Without slowing, the taillights of her red scooter disappear around a curve in the wall.

"I don't know why I'm here!" I put on more speed. "But I need to get back to the bakery!"

My chest burns, but even when I shift into hyper-speed, she remains just out of sight. I don't remember the corridor of doors being this long last time when she offered me a way back into Dreamland.

Not a lot of demons are faster than succubi and incubi, but hyper-speed comes at a high cost. The ball of energy in my belly unravels fast, the price of keeping up burning through all of my reserves. My skin begins to feel tight, my bones achy, and hunger floods through me. I stumble to a stop before I tap into the power at my core that supports my corporeal form.

Wheezing, my yell comes out as a thready rasp. "Could you slow down just a little, please?"

I brace one hand on the wall and shuffle forward. In the next instant, I almost fall flat on my face when my support disappears, spilling me out into the library.

Today, the shelves sit in deep shadow with the fitful flicker of lamp light unable to pierce the gloom. Darkness swathes the check-in desk, and the glow from the Librarian's ancient monitor casts a beacon to lead me onward. The hag already sits on her stool behind the counter, head cocked at a ninety-degree angle as she watches me.

My joints ache as I shuffle forward, arms hugged around my middle to fight off the chill. When I reach the high counter, I slump against it for support and stare into the saggy wrinkles that obscure the hag's eyes.

Unmindful of her sharp claws, I scowl at her. "Why'd you make me burn out all my energy?"

Her hooked nose twitches. "You did that on your own, girl."

"You wouldn't slow down!"

"The trip takes as long as the trip takes, no matter how much effort you put into it." Her head swivels the opposite direction, one ear resting on her shoulder. "You would have reached here in the same amount of time, even if you walked."

My eyes narrow into thin slits. "You really like messing with people, don't you?"

"*Yes*." The word holds a hiss to it, and her thick, black tongue sweeps out over her lips as if to enjoy the taste of my torment.

The right strap on my dress slips off one bony shoulder, my body now too emaciated to keep the dress in place. So much for my date with Kellen. I don't even have my cell phone to tell him I might not make it tonight. "What do you want? And how did you grab me? I was nowhere near the doorway to the attic."

Ever since I discovered the attic doorway held a portal, I avoid it.

"Haven't you ever heard the saying all doorways lead to knowledge?" She spreads her hands out. "Welcome to knowledge."

Rubbing the goose bumps from my arms, I glance around. "I'm pretty sure that's not a saying."

"Of course, it is," she insists.

"That's creepy."

"It's convenient." Her body turns to her computer while her head remains focused on me. "I need you to find a book for me."

"Umm, okay." I stare back into the shadows. "Any particular one? And why's the place so gloomy?"

"The library takes the form of the person in need of it."

My spine stiffens. "Are you saying I'm gloomy?"

She clicks her tongue. "Not everything is about you, baby succubus."

I clutch the edge of the desk to stop myself from throttling her. "Then, why am I here?"

She shrugs. "Right doorway, right time."

"Well, I'm busy, so let's make this quick." My fingers tap the hard surface. "What's the book so I can go grab it and you can send me back to the bakery?"

"Such confidence." A quiet buzz fills the room, and she reaches beneath the counter for the printout. She pushes it across the counter.

I can't read the title, but I guess it doesn't really matter. "Okay, what's the shelf location?"

She releases a put-upon sigh that stinks of stale blood. "Do you really think if it was in my library I would need you to fetch it for me?"

Irritation makes my wings shift inside my back. "Okay, then, where is it?"

"If I knew that, I wouldn't need you."

Frustrated, I drop the paper back onto the counter. "If you don't know who has the book, how am I supposed to?"

"You're supposed to look for it. This is a Quest." Under her breath, she grumbles, "What are they teaching demons these days? Pain in my ass, every one of them."

"You know I can hear you, right?" I push the paper back to her. "Find someone else."

Her arms fold under her sagging breasts in refusal. "No, you'll do."

I fold my own arms. "Why me?"

"Because it's one of your cousins who has it. Find the book, and bring it back."

"I'm not responsible for my cousins." I take a step away from the counter. "There's nothing in this for me."

She reaches beneath the counter and lifts out another book. "I have a latin copy of *Through the Window, Into the Soul*."

Suspicious, I stop my retreat. "What's that?"

"A succubi primer to power development." She waggles the book. "You want to learn faster, right?"

My hands curl into fists. The evil hag knows I do. It's a bargain I can't refuse.

"Fine." I snatch up the piece of paper. "I'll look for your book."

"Find it fast." I watch with interest as she stashes the primer away and she shakes a talon at me. "Don't think you can sneak in when I'm not looking. I'm *always* here. And we have a bargain."

My shoulders pull back. "The thought never crossed my mind."

"Sure it didn't." She waves at me. "Now, shoo. I'm busy."

The library folds in on itself, the shelves compressing in a blur until I find myself back in the hall, in front of the frosted glass door labeled Boo's Boutique Bakery. Dizzy, I throw a hand out to catch my balance as the world rights itself again. My stomach threatens to expel the food I ate earlier, and I take a moment to focus on not puking.

Once I get my body under control, I reach for the door, but it swings open on its own. Kelly bustles past, his biker physique and tattoos out of place with the hairnet on his head and beard. He carries a twenty-five pound bag of flour on one shoulder with ease. He doesn't see me as he walks past, his stride purposeful as he heads back to the kitchen.

With a deep breath, I step through the portal, the tingles itchy against my skin. The warm scent of baking desserts fills my senses, and my mouth waters. But it's not food I crave. The humans in the front of the shop call to me, happy meals on legs waiting for me to devour them.

I haven't felt hunger like this since the day I met Tobias, and I've forgotten the struggle to resist the temptation of human life force. Happiness hangs in the air and ghosts across my skin. With enough time, I could skim it and replenish my reserves. But my legs shake with the desire to hurry the process, to slake my thirst.

Kellen. I need Kellen before I hurt one of the humans. Or even more terrifying, one of my imps.

Before I give into the temptation of an easy meal, I stumble down the hall and push through the side door that leads to the alley. The sound of the door shutting behind me comes with a wave of relief. Without my purse, I can't get back inside unless I go in the front.

In the semi-darkness of the alley, I shiver. At just after seven, sunlight still fills the street, and I shuffle toward that bright sidewalk and the warmth it offers. When I join the flow of pedestrians, I make sure to keep my gaze on the sidewalk. At my current hunger level, my succubus nature might kick in and beguile the next available food source. Not something I want to risk right now. I hold my breath as much as possible and wish I still carried sunglasses to obscure my eyes.

By the time I make it to Fulcrum, I clutch my elbows to keep from latching onto the nearest human. My stomach hugs my spine, and my bones ache with a cold the sunlight can't drive away.

A line forms at the door, waiting for entry into the club, and I shuffle past it, my focus locked on the door. Through there, Kellen waits, and the knowledge makes my legs shake with desire.

A thick arm bars my path. "Back of the line, toots."

My attention shifts to the bouncer's shoulder. "I'm here to see Kellen."

"Yeah?" Derision fills his voice. "You and a hundred others. Don't get your hopes up. Boss likes them with more meat on their bones."

My fingers squeeze tighter around the knobs of my elbows. "I'm on the list."

"Not one I'm aware of." He snaps his fingers at me. "Move along."

This is so not the way tonight was supposed to go. Glancing up, I catch his eye. "Let me in."

The small push of power I put behind the word hurts, like broken glass that digs its way out through my pupils. He blinks with confusion, and for a moment, I worry I didn't use enough. But then he nods and drops his arm to let me pass.

Inside, the crush of humanity pulls at every demonic instinct inside me. So much lust, need, and desire. High passion blankets the air, hugs around me with a readiness to be consumed that's hard to resist. Only the tickle of Kellen's sigil holds me back, a warning this is protected territory.

Despite his easy-going nature, Kellen won't accept energy poaching, even from me.

Hugging the wall, I aim for the employee hallway off to one side where Kellen's office waits at the end. Will he be there? If not, I'll hole myself up there until he returns.

I make it to the hall without incident, and when no employees linger in the bright corridor to block my way, relief makes my limbs shaky. Right now, I don't think I have enough in me to whammy them to let me pass.

As I venture closer to Kellen's office, though, soft voices float back to me. "Come on, Kellen, it's been ages since we last went out. I'm beginning to think you don't like me anymore."

His light tone holds an edge of warning. "I already told you that was a one-time thing. You agreed to it then."

Anger spikes through me, not liking the sound of this conversation.

"You can't honestly say you got enough, though," the woman purrs.

I reach his office and step through the open doorway. Kellen leans against his desk, palms flat on its surface as he leans away from the blond plastered to his front. Lush curves fill out a skin tight blue dress, and her thick hair hangs down to her bubbly ass. Her toned arms twine around Kellen's neck as she stands on tiptoes to try to kiss him.

Rage turns my vision red. Mine. My meal. My storm demon. My Kellen.

He glances up, and his eyes widen to see me there. His hands lift toward the woman, but I reach her first, yanking her off of him.

"Mine," I hiss into her startled face.

Her expression morphs into instant outrage. "Now look, here, bitch. I don't know who you think you ar—"

I fist the front of Kellen's shirt. "This is mine. Never touch again."

Kellen's hand covers mine, static sinking beneath my skin in a welcome rush. "Adie—"

I twist to him. "Mine."

Lightning sparks across his pupils. "Prove it."

I don't need tiptoes. Using his collar, I yank him down to me, my mouth slamming over his.

(Un)Tethered

Distantly, the human curses angrily, but my focus pinpoints on Kellen's mouth, the hard curve of his upper lip and the softer give of the lower. Despite his immortality, laugh lines dance at the edges of his mouth, and I taste them for their happiness before skating my tongue across the warm crease of his lips.

They open instantly, and I push my way in, past the hard barrier of his teeth to the sweetness of his tongue. He drank whiskey recently, and it adds a smoky richness to his flavor. Deeper, at the back of his throat, I lap at the wellspring of crackling power. It pops against my tongue, making the fine hairs on my body rise, and I wrap my arms tighter, tilt my head for a better angle, and let his power flow into me.

It crackles its way down my throat and into my

belly, easing the ache of hunger. Greedy, my fingers thread through Kellen's red locks, alternately kneading and tugging. The ache in my bones fades, the tightness of my skin dissipating as my corporeal form regenerates.

I'm not sure how much time passes before I realize Kellen isn't participating in the kiss but simply allowing me to feed.

Unease ripples through me, and I force myself to pull my mouth from his. When my lashes flutter open, lightning blue eyes meet mine.

They skim over my face, searching, before he smiles. "You look better, but you need more."

"Kellen, who's this whore?" demands an angry voice behind me.

Surprised the human didn't already leave, I twist to glare at her. Energy sings through my veins, not as much as I'd like, but certainly enough to send her packing, never to return to Kellen. I spindle a line out, ready to whammy her, when Kellen's arms fold around me.

"This is my woman." Shocked by the declaration, I glance back at him to find his gaze hard as he stares at the human. "As I told you before, I'm no longer on the market."

Warmth spreads through my chest. I've never

been someone's woman before. Even if he's just saying it to make her go away, it fills me with excitement. I let him have the advantage and rise on my tiptoes to nuzzle his neck.

In answer, his hands move to my ass and tug me closer as he rumbles, "Close the door on your way out."

Once the door clicks closed, I move up to his ear, catching the lobe between his teeth. "So, I'm your woman?"

"You're about to be." His hold tightens as he turns, then plants me on his desk. His hips push my knees apart, his hands moving to my thighs to find bare skin and push my dress higher. "How can I resist when you come in, wearing my symbol, and lay claim to me?"

"That's not—"

His lips cut me off in a hard kiss before he pulls back to stare me in the eye. "That's exactly what you did."

"I didn't mean—"

"Hush, Adie." He tugs me closer to the edge of the desk. "Just follow your instinct. It knows what you want."

He drops to his knees in front of the desk as he pushes my dress up to my waist, exposing the thin stretch of silk that separates my core from view. My heart races as he kisses the inside of my knees, first one, then the other. He moves higher, with gentle nips and a hot slide of his tongue, covering every inch of my inner thighs. My muscles quiver, liquid heat pooling between my legs.

When he reaches my center, his warm breath fans over the damp silk, and my stomach muscles clench with anticipation. My body remembers the feel of his mouth against my folds and yearns to have him there again.

My eyes land on the new, black leather sofa against the right wall, and I lick my lips, my pulse racing. "Do you want to move to someplace where I can touch you, too?"

"No." He breathes the word against my core. "I want you on my desk, the scent of you in the wood." I shiver with want as his nose nudges against me, and he inhales. "I want to remember how you look, splayed across my desk, every time I come to work."

I lean back on my elbows and spread my legs wider. "Like this?"

He gazes up the line of my body, his voice thick with desire. "Yes."

I shrug my shoulders until the spaghetti straps slip down my arms, and the bodice of the dress slides down to the tips of my breasts, my hard nipples holding it up. "Or maybe like this?"

His mouth brushes over my core, enticing in its nearness, with only the thin piece of silk separating us. "Yes."

My hand moves to his hair to urge him closer. "Don't you want to taste me?"

His eyelashes flutter shut. "Yes."

His mouth opens over me, his tongue pressing against my underwear, making the material even more wet before he breathes against it. The dual sensation of hot, then cold, makes my muscles clench.

My breath catches as a finger slides along the edge of my underwear to push it aside. His knuckle grazes over my needy flesh, while my hand in his hair pulls him forward. He releases a low chuckle that vibrates through my body like thunder, and when his mouth touches my bare core, the static charge lifts my body from the desk. My back arches, and only his hands on my hips hold me in place as his tongue pushes into me. The dress slips to my waist, the air in the room cool against my exposed breasts.

I hook my legs over his shoulders to lock him in place as his mouth plays over me, licking at my heated flesh. His fingers move through my slick need, circling my opening before moving up to expose my clit. Warm lips gently suckle, making my hips buck as pleasure spreads through my body. I writhe beneath him, moaning his name, then cry out as his fingers plunge inside of me.

It's been so long since someone stroked inside of me, and my muscles tighten around his fingers, trying to keep him inside as he drags his fingers out, then plunges them in again. Deep inside, they make a scissor motion, stretching me for his tongue to return and delve within my body. He groans with pleasure, the vibration rolling through me to heighten my need. The stroke of his fingers and thrust of his tongue alternate until my head goes fuzzy with desire, my body tense and straining toward release.

At the edge of orgasm, he pulls back and stands. He catches my legs as they slip off his shoulders, and with one easy pull, he drags my sodden underwear off and tosses them onto the desk. My muscles clench around an aching emptiness that needs to be filled. With a whimper, I lift onto my elbows to stare as he slowly unbuckles his belt and lowers his fly.

I whimper again as he fists his hard cock and strokes its length. "You want this?"

My knees shake as I spread them wide. "Yes."

I want it with every fiber of my being. It's not even driven by hunger. Feeding sits forgotten at the back of my mind. I want Kellen's body joined with mine, to be connected with him as one being. We've danced around this moment more than once, and now, my heart races with excitement as I reach for him.

His cock fills my hand with a solid heat, and static dances along my palm and up my arm. How will he feel clenched inside my body with all of that wonderful energy pouring straight into my core?

My ankles fasten around his hips to pull him closer, and husky moans escape me at the first brush of his satiny tip against my heat. My inner muscles tremble, desperate for the stretch to come, and I look up to meet Kellen's hungry gaze as I rub him back and forth over my opening, slicking him with the combined fluids of our bodies.

His hands move to my knees, hitch me off the desk, and his tip slips past my outer folds and nudges against the tighter ring of muscles at my core.

His focus drops to where our bodies meet, then

shifts back to my face. With a low growl of thunder, he warns, "I won't be gentle."

Licking my lips, I lean back on my elbows, my body on display for him. "I won't break."

His fingers dig into my hips, yanking me forward off the desk as he seats himself to the hilt inside me. As pleasure rushes through me, my head falls back. I can't remember the last time I felt so filled, and my muscles ache at being stretched by him. He pulls back and thrusts into me again, hard enough to lift my body.

I clutch the edge of the desk, lifting myself into the next thrust, rolling my hips. I squeeze around him, and he hisses with pleasure. Power floods through my body, rolling through my core, then out to my limbs. A turbulent storm that whispers of destruction and rebirth. I struggle to reign it in, to spindle it into my core as static erupts along every inch of my skin. It crackles and sparks, a mini lightning storm that plays out over my flesh as Kellen surges into me hard and fast. My nipples ache, beaded into hard points that beg for attention, but all of Kellen's focus goes into joining our bodies together in a primal rhythm of give and take.

When my eyes shut, storm clouds roll across my eyelids. As he warned, he's not gentle, and my bones shake with the echoes of thunder. Pleasure like none I've felt before builds at my core, and my thighs tighten around him, my heels digging into his ass when he slams into me and grinds his hips, rubbing against my clit.

He pulls out and my legs tighten, forcing him back as I whimper with need. So close. As he grinds against me again, it tips me over the edge. Lightning courses through my body, my back arching off the desk. My muscles convulse around him, and he freezes, flush against me. Hot cum fills my core, bringing with it another rush of power that makes my toes curl with a second orgasm, and the edge of the desk gives with a crack as my hold tightens on it.

Panting, my eyes open again, and a haze of gray smoke fills the room, the scent of burnt wood heavy in the air. Confused, I drop the pieces of desk and turn my head to find the desktop scorched black.

"*Now* we can move to the couch," Kellen growls.

Before I can fully focus, Kellen grasps my hand and tugs me upright, his arms looping around my waist as he lifts me from the desk. His cock, still semi-hard, stays planted inside me as he strides to the couch and sits down, my knees on either side of his thighs and our bodies still locked together.

Heart still racing, tremors rattle through me, and my core flexes around him, marveling at the shape of him inside me.

His fingers nudge my chin up, and he studies me, then smiles. "Much better."

Another tremor shakes through me, and I lean forward to nip at his lips. "Thank you for the meal."

"Anytime." His hands skim over my shoulders, thumbs tracing my collarbones. "Having you fully here with me makes this so much better."

I shiver at his light caress, sad now that I can't remember the first time I held him within my body. If it was even half as good as this, I should never have waited so long. But it's better this way, after we got to know each other. After he claimed me as his woman.

He leans back, his eyes dropping to my breasts, and he traces a path over my racing heart. "What are you thinking?"

Heat rushes to my cheeks. I can't admit I like his claim. I'm already an embarrassment as a demon. Instead, I lean closer to lick his lower lip. "I'm still hungry."

A small flex of my new power brings his cock back to readiness as it hardens inside me. His eyes widen in surprise, and I flex my muscles, giving him a tight squeeze.

His hands drop to my hips, and he rolls beneath me. "Succubi are the best."

My eyes narrow at the reminder I'm not his first succubus, and I squeeze him tighter, flexing muscles human women don't possess. "Yes, succubi *are* the best."

My fingers thread through his hair, kneading against his scalp, and a groan of pleasure escapes his lips. Slowly, I curl my hands into fists, locking his head in place by his fiery strands. He stills, his expression suddenly wary.

"You're so eager to put yourself at a disadvantage," I coo as the muscles in my thighs tense. Slowly, I slide my body up his length, until only the tip of his cock remains inside me, before I sink down on him once more. "You should have more concern for your wellbeing, Storm God."

Interest sparks, little lightning bolts that skitter across his pupils as he purrs, "Will you suck me dry, little succubus?"

"Isn't that why you want me?" I undulate on top of him. "To make you safe for the human plane? So you can stay here and run your club?"

Ozone fills the air, along with the fresh scent of

rain on damp earth. His hands on my hips flex. "I think you're forgetting who you're toying with, Adie." Despite all the power he poured into me a moment ago, thunder rumbles through the air. "I can rip that summer storm right out of you. Uncreate you with a thought."

The temperature in the room drops. The lights flicker as the power surges in the club. Before he can strike, I untether my energy and sink metaphysical hooks into him. I already hold his body, his desire, within me. It's an easy thing to grasp onto the rest, to yank it into myself. He stiffens, his hips jerking up in a hard thrust, and I groan with pleasure.

My wings unfurl from my back, stretching to expand the feathers and give me added balance as I ride him. Desire and hunger roll through me.

My storm demon. No one else's. He needs to submit, to understand there will be no others in his bed. If I have to destroy him in the process, so be it.

I dive forward, mouth latching onto his, and pour my power down his throat. He comes with a harsh groan, and I wind my power tighter around him, keeping him hard. I want everything inside of him, every drop.

My hard nipples rub against the stiff material of

his dress shirt, the silk of his slacks abrasive against my thighs. The separation of skin shoots anger through me, and the shirt rends into tatters beneath my claws until my bare flesh presses against his.

The lights flicker around us, the air charged and crackling, as I reverse the direction of energy, pulling it back into myself. Greedy, my arms wind around his neck, and I abandon his mouth for the delicate skin of his throat where his artery flutters just below the surface.

He cups the back of my head, his face pressing to my ear. His voice holds the weight of tsunamis as he growls, "Are you enjoying yourself?"

Warning rings through my bones at the same time he grips my ass, pushing me down on his hard cock and taking control of the pace. I grab the back of the couch, but a jerk of his shoulder slams me onto my back, my wings caught beneath me as he presses me into the soft leather of the sofa.

With one hand on my shoulder to pin me down, he rises over me. The overhead lights flicker as if a storm fills the office. His golden muscles glisten as he shrugs out of the tattered remains of his shirt in the same moment he pushes my power aside, breaking my hold with no effort at all.

He extends the remains of his shirt. "You owe me a new one of these."

I bare my teeth at him, refusing to take responsibility.

"No?" He throws the shirt aside and slides a hand down to where our bodies connect. His thumb strokes through my folds to find the hard numb that sits at the height of my pleasure. "Should I take payment from your body?"

His hips press tight against me, his cock motionless as he circles my clit. Pleasure rushes through me, and I moan, helpless and at his mercy. How did the tables turn so fast?

Restless, my legs shift against him, thighs hugging his hips. I need friction, his cock moving within me. I need the power-laden heat of his release.

"Kellen." I reach for him, just out of touch as he pins me down.

Shadows cover his face. "Are you asking me to be gentle now? After your tried to devour me?"

My hands open and close in desperation. If I'm his woman, and not just another succubi, he'll bend his will.

With a curse, he leans over me, covering my body with his as his mouth finds mine. His body rocks into me, giving more of himself with every thrust. I wrap my arms and legs around him, murmuring my pleasure against his lips.

One hand rises to cup my breast, and he lifts it to his mouth, his tongue hot, his teeth light as he worships my flesh. My fingernails dig into his back, his biceps, his ass, every part of him I can reach, marking him.

As my body tightens, he returns to my lips, pouring power down my throat. The overhead lights dim, the office cast in near darkness. Kellen reaches once more between our bodies, his touch soft as he finds the place our bodies connect once more. With gentle caresses, he circles my clit, pushing me over the edge into orgasm. My muscles ripple around his hard length, and he groans against my mouth as his cock pulses inside me.

Pleasure drunk, my eyes flutter open to meet his in the near darkness. He brushes the hair from my face and leans down to kiss me once more, his lips feather light.

The tenderness of the gesture melts my heart. "Kellen—"

Pounding comes from the office door, followed by Slater's urgent voice. "Boss, we have a problem!"

Not a Claim

Kellen lifts onto his elbows, his weight easing from me, and barks, "Come in."

Slater pushes the door open, takes two steps inside, spots us on the couch, and scowls. "I guess I know why we're having power issues."

Beneath Kellen, I wiggle to pull my dress up, but the material's twisted and stuck between us. Poking at him, I hiss, "Get off me."

Instead, he settles more firmly between my legs. "We're not done yet."

"The hell we're not." I glance to Slater, who waits with his arms folded over his broad chest. "We're not continuing right now."

Kellen also twists enough to glare at his right hand man. "If it's just the lights, you can go."

When he leans down, his focus intent on my

mouth, I throw my hands up to cover his face. "I'm not a freaking exhibitionist! Get *off* me!"

"It's not just the lights," Slater interrupts. "We have an issue on the dance floor."

"Then deal with it," Kellen mumbles through my fingers. "I'm on a date."

My eyes narrow on him, my wings fluttering with agitation where they remain trapped between the couch and me. "This is *not* a date."

Slater growls low in his throat. "If it were that easy, I wouldn't be here."

Taking matters into my own hands, I spindle out enough power to give me added strength and shove Kellen off. I have my dress straightened and wings back in hiding before he hits the floor with a surprised grunt. I swing my legs over the edge of the couch and stand.

As I step over his prone body, his fingers curl around my ankle. "We're not done here."

"Boss, you're really needed on the floor," Slater points out.

"We're done." I stretch, enjoying the pain-free swing of my joints and the large ball of energy in my belly. "I'm full."

His hold tightens. "I can *un*fill you."

"You'll have to catch me first." I pull free of his hold easily and stride to the desk.

A scorched, Adie-shaped outline mars the polished surface, and I snatch my underwear from where they lay draped over the phone. No way I'm leaving those here for Kellen to play with. I stuff them safely into my cleavage.

When I turn, Kellen stands with his pants still unzipped, his destroyed shirt in one fist. He casts me a baleful glare, and I shrug. Nothing I can do about it now.

Slater's arms unfold. "I can get you a replacement from the staff room."

Kellen turns to him. "Do that."

As the other man strides from the room, Kellen stalks over to me. Suddenly unsure of him, I skitter back, and his face softens into an easy smile. He reaches out to catch my hand. "I'll deal with this fast, then we can continue our date. I'll have dinner delivered, and we can dance after."

"Dance?" My eyes shoot to the couch, and I lick my lips.

"I mean on the dance floor. With the humans." He tugs me closer. "That was my original plan before you showed up to lay claim on me."

Heat floods my face. "I told you, I didn't mean—"

His lips stop my words with a gentle kiss. No possession goes into it, no bid for dominance or power exchange, just a soft press of his mouth against mine. Large hands cup my head as he eases back. "Don't reject what happened here tonight. Your jealousy pleases me."

Spine stiffening, I grip his arms to push him away. "I wasn't jealous."

"Oh?' He gives me a considering look. "So, I should go get Charlotte and—"

Clutching him arms tighter, I twist and slam him backward over the desk. "Touch her, and I'll turn you to dust."

He grins. "Jealous."

Startled, I release him, then stare in horror at the red handprints on his biceps. What am I doing? He's a destruction demon. He can crush me. "Kellen, I'm *so* sorry."

"I'm not asking for an apology." He eases back into an upright position. "As I said, this development makes me happy."

Disbelief coats my throat. "You like being thrown around?"

"I like knowing you have feelings for me." His gaze heats with desire. "It makes me want to—"

"Boss, I got the shirt." Slater strides back into the room. His steps slow for a second with hesitation as he takes in our new position, then his shoulders square and he joins us at the desk. He holds out a black button-up shirt.

Lip curled with distaste, Kellen slides off the desk and accepts the shirt, slipping his arms through the sleeves. His muscles strain the seams, the shirt designed for a smaller frame, and he glances at me with annoyance once more. "You *will* compensate me for my shirt."

My hands fold behind my back. "I believe my contract stipulates I will not be held accountable for syphoning energy."

His eyes narrow. "This and that are two different things."

"Your shirt was a byproduct of syphoning and therefore falls under contract." I lift onto my toes, voice hard. "I know my contract, Kellen."

"So you do." His tone holds the caress of admiration before he turns to Slater. "What's this problem that needs my attention so urgently?"

Slater snaps to attention. "One of the VIPs is

making a scene. He's accusing the bartender of serving him cheap alcohol."

"And you couldn't take care of that yourself?" Kellen scoffs. "This is hardly worth my time."

"He's a *foreigner*." Slater's gaze slides between us with significance. "From your home country?"

I perk up with interest as Kellen swears. "Please don't say it's Domnall MacAteer."

"It's Domnall."

"Why didn't you tell me sooner?" Kellen strides for the door, his steps close to a run.

Slater and I rush after him, and I whisper, "Who's Domnall?"

"Real-estate tycoon. He owns most of the west side of the city, while Kellen owns the east," Slater whispers back as Kellen gets farther ahead of us. "They're constantly at each other's throats."

"Why would he be at Fulcrum, then?"

"Because they like to pretend they're friends." Loud music fills the hall as we near the dance floor. "Fulcrum sits on the edge of his turf. He's been trying to get his hands on it for a while now."

By the time we reach the main room, Kellen's already halfway across the room, the crowd parting before him naturally, the humans not even aware they're doing it. Unfortunately for us, they crowd closes back up as soon as he passes, forcing Slater and me to skirt the perimeter.

Instead of heading toward the bar, Slater leads the way into a roped off area next to the DJ stand. I point up at the scaffolding and shout, "Why aren't you up there?"

"I'm not on again until Saturday!"

That makes sense if Slater's one of their lead DJs. He'd get the prime time spots to keep the larger crowds going. I nod and stand on my tiptoes to see over the heads of the crowd gathered in front of the VIP area. Wannabes hover on the outskirts, dressed in revealing clothes to catch the eye of the rich patrons within. My summer dress looks out of place among all the tight, dark fabric, the swirls of *not* storm clouds glowing under the black lights that decorate the side of the staircase that leads up to the music podium.

Slater shoulders a path through them, turning a deaf ear to their protests, then their fawning when some recognize who he is and try to latch onto him in an effort to get across the velvet barrier. I mold myself to his back in an effort not to be separated, and when the bouncer raises a questioning eye at me, Slater nods to allow me to pass.

A skinny girl who can't be out of her teens tries

to do the same, her hand on my back like we come as a pair. I glare over my shoulder at her. The bouncer catches her by the scruff of the neck and tosses her back across the line.

As soon as we make it into the cordoned off area, I step out from behind Slater and glance around, curious. I haven't been to this part of the club. Set behind the DJ's speakers, the music loses some of its deafening quality. Plush, black leather couches form a circle around a large table filled with liquor glasses in varying shades of the rainbow.

Kellen stands in front of a dark-haired man who lounges in the center of the couch, directly across from us, in the most advantageous spot to view the club with minimal effort. His arms spread over the back of the couch, claiming the entire four-seater for his exclusive use. One long leg rests with his ankle propped on his opposite knee, completely relaxed.

Slater and I move to stand behind Kellen as the storm demon says, "Domnall, to what do I owe the pleasure?"

Unaffected by Kellen's looming, the other man lifts one thick eyebrow. "Kellen, so nice of you to spare some time in your busy schedule."

The muscles in Kellen's jaw jump. "I'm always available for you."

"Ever the gracious host." Domnall's eyes move past him to skim over the club. "When are you going to sell this infested warehouse to me? It would do so much better as a department store. High end fashion is where the money's at right now."

"Fulcrum is not, nor will it ever be, for sale. If that's all you came for, you can see yourself out." Kellen jerks his chin toward the exit.

Domnall's gaze lands on me, and a slow smile spreads across his lips. "Well, well, well. What do we have here? Kellen, are you finally branching out to the escort service?"

My spine snaps straight, and I take a step forward. "I'm not a prostitute, asshole."

His nostrils flare, and his leg drops to the ground as he leans forward, eyes suddenly bright with interest. "Why, no, you're not, are you? Aren't you delicious."

A possessive hand lands on my shoulder, and I glance up at Kellen, who gives me a slight shake of his head. My teeth click with irritation. I won't standby and be called a whore. I thought I made that clear early on in our relationship.

If we even have a relationship. My eyes narrow on him. "I think I'll head out now."

"Don't be in such a rush." Domnall catches my

wrist, and energy sinks fiery teeth into my bones. "Come sit next to me. I'd like to get to know you better."

Irritation rushes through me as his power wiggles its way into the rolling mass I took from Kellen earlier. Blocking off my natural ability to absorb energy, I snatch my hand back. "No, I don't think so."

Unfazed, Domall rises with a languid shift of muscle. On his feet, he stands at the same height as Kellen and several inches above me. Avarice fills the gaze he skims over my body. "I came here looking for someone else but finding one of your kind here is an added bonus."

Kellen moves to place me slightly behind himself. "Adeline is not interested in anything you have to offer. Nor is anyone else in my club. If you're hunting, you're in the wrong territory."

I'm equally annoyed Kellen chose to speak for me and flattered at the quiet growl of possessiveness in his voice. I nuzzle his shoulder in appreciation, the muscles hard beneath my cheek. He doesn't like this demon, whoever he is.

A small breeze from the overhead vents brings with it the scent of ozone and burning wood. The hint of ash makes my nose itch, and I resist the urge to rub it. He's some kind of fire demon, a big brother to Torch, only powerful enough to hold a human-shaped corporeal form on this plane.

He leans to the side to catch my attention, and a shift in the strobe lights slants across his eyes, revealing a startling shade of pale brown, almost gold. "You going to let him speak for you?"

"I can speak for myself." My chin lifts. "And I have no interest."

"But you don't even know what you're passing up," he reasons.

"I don't need to."

"She's under contract." My shoulders stiffen at that reminder from Kellen. Over the last few weeks, I thought of myself less as their contracted succubi and more as...something *more*.

"I can buy you out." Domnall steps to the side to bring us closer together. "I have need of someone of your skills. Name your price."

"Now, you're just pissing me off." I move away from both men and almost bump into Slater. He was so quiet, I forgot he was still with us. He bars my immediate exit, and I bare my teeth at him. "You joining this macho fest?"

He neatly steps to the side. "I have nothing but respect for you, Ms. Pond."

As he should. I freaking saved his job when I stopped Kellen from destroying the city during a thunderstorm, and I employ his roommate slash possible lover.

"Adie, wait." Kellen reaches for my elbow, and I slap his hand away.

"Whatever this is"—I gesture between him and Domnall—"I want nothing to do with it. This *contract* will see you later. Maybe."

Determined, he looks back at Domnall. "I don't have time for you right now. See yourself out."

"I actually did come here with something that needs your attention, old friend." Domnall steps forward, his voice dropping to a low rumble I can't pick up, even with my heightened sense.

But the effect on Kellen is instant. His face hardens, and he glances at me. "Adie, I'll see you at home later." His focus shifts to Slater. "See that she gets back to her car safely."

Alarm rattles my bones. "What's going on?"

"Not now." And with that, Kellen turns his back on me.

I waffle between staying to discover what's happening and storming out of the club. This is *not* how tonight was supposed to go.

"There's a side exit." Slater gestures to a wall

covered by black curtains farther back in the VIP section. "It leads to the back parking lot."

"I didn't drive here." With one last glance at the two demons huddled together, I stomp in the direction he indicated. "I can get back to the bakery by myself."

Doggedly, he stays on my heels. "I'll walk you."

I glare over my shoulder at him. "You know I can ditch you in an instant, right?"

His jaw sets in a stubborn line. "I'm aware, but I'd appreciate it if you didn't. I don't need Kellen angry at me for not following orders."

I remember Kellen's statement about owning Slater, and some of the anger dissipates. I shouldn't take it out on him just because my date went sour. My steps slow enough that Slater doesn't have to hurry to keep up.

As we reach the curtain and he holds one side open to reveal a door, I mutter, "Sorry."

"They're both being assholes." He cuts a glance at me from the corner of his eye. "Nothing new, right?"

The memory of Kellen's tenderness in his office jumps to the forefront of my mind, and I push it aside with a decisive nod. "Right."

We step outside into the setting sun, and I peer

up at the pink tinted sky in surprise. Was I really only in there for less than two hours? It felt longer. The summer heat turned chilly while inside the club, and now, I shiver in my new summer dress. Nothing to be done about it, though.

Turning, I set off in the direction of the bakery, Slater at my side.

Where There's Smoke

"So, how'd you meet Kellen?" I ask, after we walk a bit in awkward silence.

While I've met all of Tally's roommates on multiple occasions, I've never really talked to them. One of them is always at the bakery, keeping an eye on Tally, and I can't decide if it's because they can't bear to be separated from her, they're still suspicious I'll try to feed off her, or if Tally's in some kind of danger.

Her constant, upbeat mood makes me think she's *not* in danger, but maybe that's a side effect of eating too many happy people's dreams? Baku demons usually feed on nightmares. What kind of genetic side effects might come from Tally going against the nature of her kind?

Slater stays quiet for long enough I think he might not answer, and I probably shouldn't have asked. The relationship he has with Kellen isn't any of my business, and after Kellen's declaration of ownership this morning, it might be a touchy subject for Slater.

The way humans become owned by demons is varied and usually circles around dealings gone wrong. Were Slater and the others in a cult? Did they sign a bad contract with Kellen that cost them their souls?

Demons don't really harvest souls. At least, most don't. Succubi kind of do, if we feed too much, but that's different. It's not like we're tormenting the souls for eternity. We just eat them.

Slater's deep voice breaks me out of my own thoughts. "He helped us out when we were kids. Jax and I were in a bad spot, and Kellen stepped in. We owe him."

I glance at him from the corner of my eye. Owing Kellen and being owned by him are two completely different things. Was Kellen messing with me earlier, or is it possible Slater doesn't know the full extent of his debt to the storm demon? Or am I putting my nose where it doesn't belong and Slater doesn't want to admit to being owned?

The muscles in Slater's jaw jump as he clenches and unclenches his teeth, and I decide it's not my business, as curious as I am to know more. "So, you and Tally. Did Kellen introduce you?"

A smile ticks at the corner of his lips. "No, she came to us on her own."

Flickering light catches my attention as we walk past a dress shop, and I turn my head to stare at the door. Sparkles of light shoot along the frame, and my skin itches with the nearness of a portal. As we walk past, the sparkles disappear, only to appear on the next door ahead of us, and I swear under my breath.

Slater glances at me in surprise. "Something wrong?"

"Just someone being impatient." I move closer to the street, away from the portal that now lines the cell phone shop's door, and bump into Slater. Caught mid-step, he stumbles to the side and catches himself against an electric signboard.

Embarrassed, I catch his arm. "Sorry about that."

"No prob." He straightens, rolling his shoulders, and the faint scent of ozone comes from the leather cord around his neck.

I reach up to tap it, and he flinches away, bumping into the billboard once more. My hand drops to my side. "Sorry, it's just..." I lean close to sniff the air next to him. "You know what you smell like, right?"

His large hand covers the front of his shirt, over a small bump in the fabric. "Yeah, I know."

My brows wrinkle with concern. "You might draw the wrong kind of attention wearing that."

His dark brown eyes harden. "I know the danger."

Well, I guess it's his risk to take, drawing the attention of other demons. The sign behind him shifts to display rows of books and computer tables. At the top, it reads *Visit your local library to expand your view*.

Glaring at the sign, I mutter, "I get it, hag. It hasn't even been twenty-four hours."

"What?" Confused, Slater twists to stare at the sign. "Oh, yeah, I heard they redid the Jefferson Library. I haven't been there in a while."

"That's not it." The sign changes again to show children sitting in a circle with a teacher reading a picture book to them. And beneath that, in small script, *Books are the gateways to new worlds*.

I reach past Slater to jab at the sign. "That's not going to make me find it faster."

Static nips at my finger, and I jerk it back.

"Uh, Adie?" Slater shuffles out from between the sign and me. "You okay?"

"Just someone pestering me."

In answer, the sign switches to an ad for a heavy metal band, the lead singer's middle finger is pixelated out as he flips off a crowd of cheering fans.

"Yeah? Right back at you, hag!" I flip the sign off with both hands. "I'm working on it."

The sign switches over to a dripping faucet. *Are parts of your house running slower than you'd like?* Followed by a phone number.

"Ugh!" I turn away, grab Slater's arm, and hustle him along. "You have any annoying relatives?"

"No." His short answer holds the weight of stories.

My pace slows, and I release him. "Sorry, I'm being rude." I glance over my shoulder at the sign, which now displays a boring ad for car insurance. "I was assigned a task by someone who's difficult to refuse, and they're being persistent."

"How long have you been working on it?"

I nibble my lip. "Maybe two hours?"

"Sounds rough."

We lapse back into silence. I don't know why Kellen insisted Slater walk me back. I'm a demon and far more capable of protecting myself than a human. I eye the tight fit of Slater's t-shirt. No matter how buff that human is.

Uneasiness creeps along my bones, and my steps slow. It's the same feeling I had at the bakery this afternoon. Unsure where the feeling originates, I glance around casually to see if I recognize anyone from my shop earlier.

Beside me, Slater stiffens, and then his hand touches the small of my back. "We should hurry."

Surprised, I peer up at him. "What's wrong?"

He rolls his shoulders as if to dislodge a weight. "The streets aren't safe at night."

"The crime rate in our town is minimal, right?" But I don't slow our pace as we near the turn onto the street where Boo's Boutique Bakery resides. The unease heightens to rattle my bones with the alarm of imminent danger.

Slater's lips press together as he glances over his shoulder to search the crowd. His free hand creeps up to his neck, to the clay disk that holds the hint of demonic power.

"Do you know something I don't?" I hiss.

"I'm not sure." He nudges me closer to the row of shops and away from the street, putting himself between me and the other pedestrians that walk past, oblivious in their little bubbles of life. "I don't have a good sense for these kinds of things."

"What kinds of things?" Danger rattles my bones, and I spindle out some of my new power to add strength to my limbs.

Slater's hand clamps down hard on my arm. "Stop doing whatever you're doing."

Astonished, my grip on the energy slips and it sinks back to my core. "What?"

He releases me to rub his hand against his jean clad thigh. "It makes you...brighter?" He shrugs. "I don't know. Reese is bad at explaining things."

"What are you talking about?"

His eyes skip ahead. "We're almost to your shop. You have a ward or something, right? You have your territory marked or something?"

"Yeah, I have my territory marked or *something*," I hiss in frustration.

Tension keeps his shoulders tight. "Is Reese at the shop tonight?"

Bewildered, I shake my head. "No, Xander is."

"Shit. He's not as good." A tall man in a trench coat marches past, and Slater's gaze locks on him with suspicion. As it should. It's way too warm, even at night, for a trench coat. But the man passes without attacking or flashing us.

"Not as good at *what?*" Alarm ripples through me, unrelated to the sense of danger that pushes me to move fast, to abandon the human and protect myself. I clamp onto Slater's bicep, and he winces with pain. "Is this related to—" I wave my fingers in front of my eyes.

Reese, the quietest of Tally's roommates, is fairy touched, meaning he can see past the veil that protects demons from human view most of the time. Most of his kind become demon Hunters, tracking down my kind for body parts they can use in magical rituals. Reese—I've been assured on more than one occasion—isn't like that. But it's difficult sometimes to overcome decades of prejudice against his kind.

"Yes? Maybe? No?" Slater huffs out a frustrated breath. "I don't know. It might not be anything."

"If it helps, my instincts are telling me to leave you to the wolves and run."

"That...helps a little." He eases my fingers from his arm. "At least I know I'm not imagining things. And, thank you for not abandoning me."

Unable to resist, I twist to peer behind us. No one looks suspicious or has an arrow over their head flashing *evil intentions*. "I'll protect you if we're attacked."

"Thanks," he grunts. "I got your back, too."

My wings rustle against my spine, alerting me to imminent danger, and I shake my head. "If it comes to a fight, you should run."

"Kellen would flay me alive." His tone holds a serious edge, as if he knows his words to be more than a figure of speech.

"Yeah, he would." The sign over Boo's Boutique Bakery comes into view, its curly lettering and pink cupcake beckoning us to the relative safety of my wards.

In grim silence, we all but run for the front door.

The shadows of an alley separate us from the entrance, and shivers of warning crawl across my skin. They creep out to form a dark triangle on the sidewalk, untouched by the lights in front of the stores or from the street. As my foot touches one, a hand reaches out and latches onto my arm.

With a hard yank, I'm pulled into the alley, Slater tumbling after me by his hold on my waist. A dark figure looms in front of us.

Slater lunges in front of me, his arms thrown wide. "Adie, run!"

"Move out of the way, Slater!" I yell as I try to fling myself forward to protect the human.

The shadowed figure swats Slater aside with

ease, sending the large man down to one knee before it reaches for me once more. I dodge, but Slater's in my way, and strong hands latch onto me. The scent of burning wood fills the alley, curling around a strong smell of ozone. Demon.

My nostrils quiver. A demon I recognize.

"Domnall?" How the hell did he get here before us? We just left him at Fulcrum.

"You recognize me. Good. That will make this easier." He drags me past Slater, who shakes his head in confusion. I catch the coppery tinge of blood in the air, and worry shoots through me, followed fast by anger.

Energy floods my limbs, my wings bursting from my back as I shove against Domnall. My fingernails hook into the exposed flesh of his arms, and I tear into him. He shakes me off with a shout, and the air in the alley heats, a hot breeze carrying with it the burn of a forest fire. My skin tightens on my bones, screaming with the first burn of blisters.

Slater groans, covering his head even as he struggles to his feet and wavers toward us with one unsteady step.

"Slater, stay back!" I yell and smoke clogs my throat.

Coughs wrack my body, my lungs on fire as

Domnall slams me against the cement wall. My wings flutter, ineffectual as he traps me in place. His body presses to mine in a rush of fire, and I scream in pain. This is nothing like the burn of Tobias's passion and anger, or the bone melting heat of Torch's love. This fire crackles along my flesh in a devouring rush that threatens to consume me whole.

A hand grabs my jaw, forcing my head up, and I push at his shoulders. My strength means nothing against his, and he presses closer with the inevitability of death. I never thought this is how I'd end. Throttled by Tobias, sure, but not burnt to a crisp in an alley next to my bakery.

My grip shifts to his face, struggling to shove him away as he bends close enough that his hot exhale blows smoke into my face. Another cough shakes through me, and his mouth covers mine, blistering my lips. Ash funnels down my throat, and I choke, unable to breathe as the world goes dark.

(UN)PROTECTED

Distantly, Slater's loud curse reaches me and then the pound of feet against pavement as he runs away. Good for him. At least one of us will survive tonight.

Ash fills my stomach and sticks in my throat as I struggle weakly against Domnall's hold. My wings flap once, then still, and Domnall pulls me from the wall, tucking me closer to his scorching body, almost gentle in his embrace.

I blink, trying to clear the black film from my eyes, and light fingers caress my cheek, nudging my mouth wider.

Quick footsteps return to the alley, more than one set, and strange words fill my ears. They slip and slide against each other, just out of the reach of comprehension.

With a pained growl, Domnall's mouth rips from

mine, and he drops me. I land heavily against the hard cement of the alley, and my vision clears. Blinking, I focus on Xander who stands at the entrance to the alley, Slater at his side. Xander holds his laptop in front of him, oily words sliding past his lips as he focuses on the fire demon.

Tingles brush against my skin in a prickly search before they move past me, and Domnall grunts once more with pain. Peering over my shoulder, I crawl away from the enraged scowl on his face.

"Children should not play with such dangerous toys," he hisses, and smoke drifts from the edge of his lips.

Xander's voice rises, and he moves the laptop to one hand as he makes a circle and push motion with his other hand. My eyes widen in shock. Is he seriously attempting to *banish* Domnall?

Fuck.

My wings snap back into alertness, and energy floods my limbs as I spring toward the humans in hyper-speed. Xander's spell slicks my skin in oil and slides off, not intended for me. I grab both men, flee from the alley and into the bakery, where I rush through the half empty shop, the customers only registering our passing as a slight breeze.

In the kitchen, I slam to a stop and prop

Xander and Slater against the center island, in too much of a hurry to wait while they regain their bearings. I rush back to the two-way door and slap my palm over a frosting-shaped swirl etched into the wall.

Power rushes out to leave me light headed as my barriers slam into place.

A moment later, Tally runs into the kitchen, and the door slams into my back. Her voice pitches high with fear. "What is happening?"

I shove the door closed once more. My voice comes out rough and weak through the burns in my throat. "Tally, please bring the imps to the kitchen and tell the customers we're closing early for the day."

Her face pales, but she walks back through the door and her calm voice filters through the passthrough. "I'm sorry, everyone, but we have an unexpected emergency and request that you please leave. Here are coupons for a free cupcake at your next visit. Please come again."

While she speaks, Iris and Kelly join us in the kitchen, eyes wide with fright. Despite their physical differences, the two imps huddle together, chittering quietly. The others creep closer to them to form a group, with their smallest at the center.

Martha pulls a pink sparkle ball from her pocket and squeezes it, as if it will ward off the danger.

Nausea rolls my stomach, and cold sweat breaks out across my forehead. My skin feels tight with heat, but chills wrack my body. I fist a hand over my stomach where the foreign ball of energy at my core roils.

Tally returns to the kitchen after a few minutes, her gaze shifting between me and the guys. She hesitates, uncertain who to go to.

The energy inside me swells, and I stumble to the counter for support. "Tally, can you—" Pain lances through me, and I gasp for breath, struggling to focus. "Tally, Torch's box. Take him to the pantry."

"Adie, what's going on?" Fear fills her voice as she hurries to the storage rack and pulls out a heat-proof box from the bottom shelf.

"He can't—Ah!" The power spikes, pushing outward within my skin. "Get him out of here!"

Frantic, she runs to the oven and pops open the hatch, grabbing the little ignis demon with her bare hands. He flickers red and orange with worry before she stuffs him in the box and shoves it into Slater's surprised hands. "Take him to the back, and shut yourself inside."

Slater's gaze shifts between her and where I slump, panting against the counter. "Tally—"

"Now is not the time to argue!" She grabs Xander's arm and shoves the two humans toward the back hallway. "Go now! I will let you know when it is safe."

My stomach rolls, and fire creeps up my throat. I lunge for the stainless steel sink, gripping the cold surface. Down the hall, the pantry door shuts, and relief makes my limbs tremble.

Tally rushes to my side, her hands freezing against my bare skin. "Adie, what can I do?"

"Hold my hair," I gasp and lean over the sink, mouth open wide.

Black sludge pours out, scraping like glass as it rushes from my body. It glops into the basin like tar, steam rising from the mess. It slithers toward the edges, tendrils of black goo lifting to investigate the height of the steel walls. Power floods the room in a hot rush of smoke that hazes the air. I heave again, and more sludge comes out. It stinks of wet ash, of forest fires after a heavy rain.

"Fucking"—I heave again—"destruction"— more tar, a thinner stream this time—"demon."

Tally's cool hand scoops the hair off my neck,

her voice whispering with the darkness of nightmares. "One of your men did this to you?"

I shake my head, unable to speak as I heave again, but nothing comes out this time. Weak, I reach for the faucet, and the sludge hisses and boils as cold water hits it. I scoop cold water into my mouth, rinsing out the ashy residue, and spit out gray liquid. I repeat until the water turns clear, and my mouth tastes less like burnt wood, then shuffle away from the sink.

Tally takes over, grabbing the faucet wand and aiming it at the corners of the sink until all of the sludge vanishes down the drain. She leaves the water running to wash it all the way out of our pipes before she turns to me with concern.

"There are blisters." Her hand lifts to her mouth. "I will call Emil. He will help with this burn."

Emil. I want him. I want to curl up in his frosty embrace and let him soothe the ache from my body. I want to lick him until my tongue goes numb, and I can no longer feel the invasion of ash in my stomach.

But I shake my head. "You can't."

"Kellen, then? Or Tobias?" She reaches for her phone. "One of them will care for you."

I shake my head harder, and the room shifts. "They can't know."

"What? Why?" Her hand clenches around her phone. "They will not tolerate what has been done to you. They will want vengeance."

Unsteady, I sink to the floor, my legs sprawled out in front of me. I glare up at her. "The vengeance is mine."

"But..." She nibbles her lower lip. "This destruction demon who is not one of your men. He is much stronger than you."

Weakly, I smooth down the hem of my scorched dress. The pretty white swirls flake away beneath my fingertips. "They can't know."

"But, why?" Bewilderment fills her voice. "Do not let pride put you in danger."

I lean my head back against the bank of cabinets and close my eyes. "Tally, Slater was entrusted with my safety. Kellen will kill him."

"But—" Her feet shuffle, and I crack my eyes open to find her crouched in front of me. "But Xander saved you."

"Yes." I lick my lips and they sting with fine cracks. "But Slater did not."

She shakes her head. "But Slater was the one who fetched Xander."

"Slater left me in the alley with the demon." I force myself to straighten, my expression serious. "I told him to run, but it won't matter, Tally. He failed to protect me himself."

"But, he's *human*."

I remember the way he felt the danger, his muttered words about not being as good at sensing those kinds of things. Humans as a species can't do that.

"No, he's not." Her eyes widen in shocked understanding, and I nod. "At least not fully. And it wouldn't matter, even if he were. Kellen gave him a task, and he failed."

"And you would protect Slater. Even though he is not yours."

I reach for her hand, squeezing her fingers. "He's yours, though, and you're my friend."

Tears shimmer over her mahogany eyes, and she blinks rapidly before she gives a quick nod. "Then we must clean this mess up." She waves at the haze in the air. "Will this dissipate on its own?"

The power that hangs in the air ghosts along my skin, seeking entry back into my body, and I firmly shut off that part of my nature that absorbs energy. No way is that getting back inside me. "Once we're sure he's gone, we can open the doors and air it out.

You can tell the guys it's safe to come out, but leave Torch in the pantry. We can't risk him feeding on this and getting too big for his oven again."

"Right."

As she pushes to her feet, I close my eyes once more. I just need to rest a little, give my body time to sort itself out. The energy Domnall forced into me came too fast, with an almost desperate push to free himself of it. Was he like my guys and in need of a succubus to drain off his powers? I'm not the only one of my kind in town, but now that I think of it, most of my cousins live in Kellen's territory.

And none of them would be as stupid as me to take on destruction demons. I knew the job was dangerous, but I didn't realize until tonight how much restraint the guys showed when dealing with me. Domnall treated me like an empty vessel to dump his power into, while the guys let me feed at my own pace, even when it's not the best course of action for them.

My hands curl into fists. Domnall will pay for his actions.

A warm body presses against my side, and my eyes snap open, head turning to find Iris on the floor next to me. Another body presses in on my other side as Kelly settles down. The others follow until

I'm surrounded in a baby powder scented circle of imps. Even the smallest one, the one who still retains its imp form, joins the circle. It hesitantly crawls into my lap, its body light and soft as it settles against me.

They start up a quiet hum that vibrates my bones and eases the tension from my muscles.

I blink in surprise, then blink again as my eyelids grow heavy. Huh, who knew imps could be so cuddly? This reminds me of my pillow nest at home. My arms wrap around the one in my lap, and the humming changes pitch. I yawn, and Iris supports my weight as I lean more heavily against her.

When I wake up, I need to remember to ask about what Xander was doing with that laptop. Is that some new form of spellcraft? Modern witches sure know how to get with the times.

And why didn't Tally tell me her men were witches?

Shower Time

"Adie, wake up."

Grumbling, I hug the warm body in my arms and bury my nose in the soft hair behind the imps ear. The scent of baby powder is stronger here, soothing the itchy burns inside me.

"Adie, it's three in the morning. If you don't go home, your men will worry."

I crack an eyelid open to glare at Tally. She hovers over me, her pink hair turned into a glowing halo of cotton candy by the overhead lights. Imp bodies drape over me in a living blanket of soothing warmth. They more than make up for the hard tiles that press into my hip. "I'm good here. You go home."

She huffs out a breath. "But Philip is here to retrieve the imps."

My arms tighten around the one in my arms. "Mine."

The hum takes on a contented tone, and a soft hand strokes my head.

Tally bites her lip as she glances over her shoulder to the back hall. Her voice drops to a whisper, "They are contracted with Julian."

The reminder grates across my already raw nerves. "They're contracted with me, too."

"But with Julian first." Philip's young face appears behind Tally, his brown eyes too large in his narrow face. He claps his hands. "Time to go."

The hum turns to a disgruntled rumble and the imps slowly move to uncover me. The one in my arms burrows closer with a plaintive chitter. I don't want to force it to leave, but see no way around it. Philip's right. They're not mine first, and I can't currently afford to buy their contracts.

Petting its back, I slowly sit up, then struggle to my feet.

I catch Philip's eye. "Is Julian at the office today?"

"He should be in around noon." He pulls out his phone to check. "We have a couple gigs booked for later in the day."

I'm usually getting ready for work around that

time, but I can skimp on sleep today since I just had a long nap. "Okay, I'll be by to speak with him."

Reluctant, I pass the small imp to Kelly, who lifts it with ease and pats the back of its head in comfort. Next to Philip, Tally's hands open and close, the air shimmering with the hint of gossamer wings, but she steps to the side and watches in silence as the imps file out of the kitchen and into the chilly darkness of the alley.

When the door closes, she turns to me. "I wish to do something for them."

"Me, too." I scrub a hand over my face, stopping at my lips. They tingle with the thinness of new skin, and I don't feel any blisters. My hand drops to my side, and I stare at the closed door as tears sting my eyes. "I'm already in so much debt right now. Unless Julian gives me their contract for free…"

"If he knows you want it, it will cost you much."

"Yeah." I take in the air in the kitchen, now free of smoke. "Did you air the place out already? How did you know it was safe?" My brow wrinkles in confusion. "Wait, how did Philip get inside?"

My wards should still be in place, barring demons from crossing into or out of the building.

She fidgets with the buttons on her chef's coat

for a moment before sighing. "The wards went down as soon as you fell asleep."

"Seriously?" My shoulders slump in defeat. "Am I really that bad at this?"

"No one tried to enter, so we figured that meant it was safe." She walks to the passthrough and stares out to the front of the shop. "Slater returned to the club. I made him leave. Otherwise, it would have piqued Kellen's interest."

"Xander's still here, though?" I join her at the counter and discover the front of the shop empty. "Where's Xander?"

Except for our girls' shopping trip, Tally's never been left alone with me before. Her men stick to her like glue, coming to the shop every day and taking ownership of one of my smaller booths.

"I sent him away. He was angry." She glances at me from the corner of her eye. "I did not know if you would still welcome him."

I scrape my hair away from my face, the white strands slick between my fingers. "Are they all witches?"

"To one degree or another." She spins to face me and grabs my hand, her expression earnest. "They are good men. They can be trusted."

The puzzle pieces fall into place. "And they're

how you're here? How you're not trapped in Dreamland with the rest of the baku?"

Thick lashes shutter her gaze. "That is not something I can speak of."

"Kellen knows."

It's not a question. Of course, Kellen would know. He owns them. He owns a freaking quartet of witches. Does he have others stashed away somewhere? An entire coven of them? Kellen's playing a dangerous game. If the higher ups get wind of this...

My tongue clicks against the roof of my mouth. This would be a powerful bargaining chip to hold over the storm demon, but the idea of using it makes me feel slimy inside, ashamed the thought even crossed my mind.

Tally's voice comes out quiet and hesitant with worry. "Adie, will you tell?"

I roll my shoulders and push away the persuasive whispers. "Nothing to tell, right?"

She sags with relief. "Come, I will walk you to your car."

"I should stay and clean up." I glance around the kitchen to find it sparkling, every surface wiped down. Walking to the sink, I stare down at the freshly scrubbed stainless steel basin. "Or not."

"The imps took turns cleaning." She touches my elbow. "Come, let us not linger here today."

I feel it, too. The desire to leave. It hangs over the shop and obscures all the happy emotions that I worked so hard to cultivate. I curse under my breath. This won't do. This level of negativity will drive even the instinct stunted humans away. But there's nothing I can do for tonight.

I peek at Tally. "I don't suppose you know anyone who can do a cleansing?"

She perks up. "I might!"

I don't ask which of her men her thoughts zero in on. I don't want to know which of them is the most powerful, though a pair of dual colored eyes float through my memory. I shake my head to dispel the image of Reese, the quiet, fae touched man.

Nope, not going to think about it.

∽

When I get home, I half expect to find Kellen in the kitchen. Disappointment slows my steps when I find the room empty. Not that I should see him right now. I stink and, if I want to keep Slater safe, I need to scrub this smell off me before I see the guys again, or they'll ask questions I can't answer.

A chilly blast of air hits me as I open the fridge. I haven't eaten since Tally and I had lunch, but my stomach rolls at the idea of food. Maybe once I've slept for a bit.

But my body feels restless, tired yet full of energy. Sleeping at the shop for a few hours threw off my routine, and I'm unsure if I'll be able to stay still long enough to drift off.

Quiet, I tiptoe up the stairs, skipping over the fifth one that creaks. Sometimes Tac hears me come home and lets himself out of Emil's room. I don't know if it wakes the ice demon up when he does that and don't want to disturb him right now. Nothing worse than waking up before the alarm clock goes off in the morning.

Despite my best efforts, the door on the second story landing creaks open before I reach the top.

"Go back to bed, Tac," I whisper as I step onto the landing.

Instead of the monster cat, Emil's sleepy voice fills the hall. "Why are you home late?"

I jump in surprise, a hand flying over my racing heart as I spin to face his bedroom. Emil stands in his doorway, a pair of light-gray sweatpants riding low on his hips. The smooth, muscular valley of his abs and chest draw my eye, like ridges of vanilla ice cream. My mouth waters. The urge to curl up with him, to lick the dips and rises of his body, surges back to life.

I lick my lips, and pull my gaze away. "Philip was late picking the imps up." The lie feels sticky in my mouth, and I walk backward toward the bathroom, voice quiet. "Sorry if I woke you. You can go back to sleep."

Instead, he ventures farther into the hall and sniffs the air. "Did you have a fire at the bakery?" He sounds more alert now.

Crap. I need to get away from him. "Everything's fine. No need to worry."

"I'm not worried." Frost coats his voice, and I shiver. It makes me yearn for snowflakes against my skin, for ice in my bones. "Why aren't you looking at me?"

"What are you talking about?" I force my gaze up to his. "I'm looking at you just fine."

"You're hiding something." He sniffs the air, and his lip curls with distaste. "Why do you smell like baby powder?"

My shoulders hunch. "I have a lot of imps at the shop."

His nose wrinkles. "Their scent is clinging to you more than usual." He walks closer, and I scuttle into the bathroom as ice coats his expression. "Did you feed on one of them today?"

Spine snapping straight, my hands move to my hips with affront. "Of course not. I wouldn't abuse them like that."

His frosty eyes drop to my scorched dress. "What are you wearing?"

Over his shoulder, Tac appears in his doorway, blinking saucer sized green eyes. The flaps on his nostrils ruffle, and he lets out a low growl. Double crap.

Before he joins Emil in the hall, I take a large step to cross into the bathroom and grab the door. "I'm just going to shower and go to bed. Sorry I disturbed you both!"

I slam the door in Emil's startled face and snap the lock in place. Not that it will stop Emil if he really wants in. As if to backup my thought, the wood rattles in the frame, and another growl comes from the other side.

Emil's quiet voice follows. "Ms. Pond. Are you trying to hide something from me?"

"Nope!" I yank the shower curtain open, jump into the cast iron tub fully clothed, and twist on the faucets.

Cold water splashes down my back and I yelp.

While I might welcome Emil's frosty embrace, a cold shower is an entirely different beast. I turn the lever all the way to right, then cringe when the hot water hits my new skin. Swearing, I fuss with it until a tolerable lukewarm comes out of the shower head.

Over the running water, the bathroom door rattles again, and I poke my head out to yell, "Go back to bed, Tac!"

The scent in the bathroom reminds me of a damp campfire and powder, an odd combination that makes me sneeze. I push the dress off my shoulders and chuck it out of the shower, where it lands in a sodden heap halfway in the sink. Water drips onto the tiles, and I poke a leg out to push the shower mat out of range of the growing puddle. Nothing worse than a soggy bath mat.

Hopefully, there's enough towels in here to clean up the mess I'm making. Emil hates dirty bathrooms, and I already pushed my luck with the new over-the-toilet organizer I installed while he was at work one day.

But a girl needs a place to stash her personal bathroom items. A pedestal sink just doesn't cut it, and he already took over the mirrored medicine cabinet. How many bath bombs does a demon seriously need? The man's obsessed.

I duck back into the shower and tip the water closer to the warm side now that my sensitive skin has had time to adjust to the temperature. Staring down at my body, I find patches of pale skin dotted through a network of shiny new pink. How did my dress not catch on fire through all that heat? I press on my stomach and feel an answering ache inside. Or was I burning from the inside out?

I shudder at the thought, grateful that Xander was there to stop Domnall, however foolhardy his attempt may have been. The realization of what could have happened slams into me with a weight that brings me to my knees. Domnall could have killed me. Was that his aim or just a byproduct of dumping his power into me?

How is he on the human plane if he can't control his destructive powers? Is he like the guys and had a succubus or incubus helping to syphon off the excess? Did he kill his succubus? I shiver at the thought. If what I experienced tonight is a sample of his power, it's entirely possible.

If not for my recent feeding with Kellen, I might not have recovered, even with the imps' help.

I grab the shampoo bottle with shaky hands,

trying to block the memory of ash flooding my body, of having the air blocked from my lungs. Succubi are designed to feed on energy, but the way Domnall dumped it into me against my will...

I shudder with revulsion. Energy shouldn't be forced, as my body's immediate rejection showed. Until today, I never realized that could happen. I always assumed energy was energy, food was food. Learn something new every day.

Tipping my head back, I open my mouth and let water stream down my throat to wash away the phantom taste of ash.

I shampoo, rinse, and repeat until my scalp tingles, then scrub down the rest of my body. By the time I'm done, all of my skin has a rosy glow to it, and the apple fragrance of the soap masks Domnall's and the imps' scent.

Turning off the water, I push the shower curtain aside and let out a high-pitched shriek.

Emil sits on the toilet lid, his legs crossed at the knees, one elbow on the sink. My sodden dress now rests fully within the basin, and a fluffy white towel hangs from the hook on the back of the door, the tiles freshly dried.

One white eyebrow lifts as I fling my arms over myself in a completely pointless effort to hide my nudity. Frost coats his voice. "Why so shy all of a sudden?"

I've never felt a need to hide my body from them before, but some small part of me believes Domnall's imprint will be visible on my flesh. I scowl at him to hide my anxiety. "A little privacy would be nice."

"This is a shared bathroom." His nose lifts into the air. "I can enter when I please."

"Waiting your turn is the polite thing to do." I shuffle inside the claw footed tub. The dry towels hang on the wall next to him, and reaching for one will put me at a disadvantage.

He stands, and the warm air between us turns to fog. Leaning close, he inhales over the pounding pulse in my neck. "You were with Kellen tonight." Another deep breath. "But you smell weak. Why do you smell weak, Adeline?"

I shiver as crystals form along my skin. "Stop sniffing me."

Unswayed, he reaches for the wet hair draped over one breast and lifts it to his nose. "And why do you smell of another demon?"

Ice coats the blue tips of my hair, forming a frozen ring around his fingers. I lick my lips and taste a blizzard sweeping down from the mountains.

The air in the bathroom holds weight, the natural sounds dampened to dull echoes.

When Emil's gaze shifts back to meet mine, the color slowly fades, as if a snow storm masks his eyes. "Tell me about your day."

"I'd rather not." I edge to one side of the tub, then the other, but Emil effectively blocks me in. I can't climb out unless he moves.

"Do you have something to hide?" His head tilts to one side with the crackle of breaking ice. "Did you feed on another demon? Are you...unsatisfied with your current options?"

"No, I'm very satisfied." A shiver rattles through me, and I take the risk to lean past him and grab the towel. More frost forms along my skin, and I wrap the fluffy white cotton around my shoulders. Peeking back at him, my voice quiets. "I'm not cheating on you guys, if that's what you're thinking."

Blue returns to his eyes in a slow bloom of color. "Cheating implies a relationship of some sort. Are we in a relationship?"

Wings rustling with sudden nervousness, my tongue darts out to taste the air again, but his emotions are impossible to gauge. If I claim a relationship first, does it make me the weaker one? But after our date at the Italian restaurant...

I square my shoulders. "Yes, we're in a relationship of some sort."

"Hmm." The blue becomes warmer as he reaches for another towel and gently folds it around my head. "I believe relationships involve not lying to each other."

The towel covers my face for a moment as he pats at my cheeks, and I blindly reach out to grab his wrists and pull this hands down. "I'm not lying. I didn't feed on another demon."

In an instant, the temperature drops once more. "And yet you smell like you did. Does that mean someone forced their energy on you?"

I rise onto my toes. With the added height of the bathtub, it puts me at the advantage to look down at him. "I'm not weak."

"You will tell me about this later." He steps off to the side and extends a hand to help me out of the shower. "Come join me for the rest of the night."

My hand freezes above his, a snowflake's breadth from his palm. "You want sex? Now?"

White eyebrows lift. "Are you offering?"

I catch my bottom lip between my teeth and shake my head.

"Then come to sleep." He closes the distance and wraps his fingers around mine. "I have three more hours before my alarm goes off. And I would like to spend it next to you."

"Okay." Despite his icy temperature, warmth fills my chest. "I'd like that, too."

Holding my hand, he pulls me from the bathroom and down the short hall toward his room.

As we pass the staircase, my steps slow. "I should go get some pajamas."

He tugs me past. "I have plenty of blankets and pillows."

When we enter his room, my bare feet sink into the plush carpet, and heat envelopes us. A fire burns along one wall, and space heaters quietly *whir* in the corners. Tac's head pokes up from the other side of Emil's bed, his tufted ears swiveling, and a quiet growl lifts his lips.

I freeze, unsure I want to venture closer to the giant beast. "Why's he doing that?"

"He doesn't like the scent of another demon on you." Emil pulls me closer to the mound of blankets that cover his mattress. "Neither do I, but it will fade."

Releasing my hand, he folds back the blankets, then gathers the pillows that rest against the headboard and lines them up along the far side, effectively blocking Tac from view.

He glances back at me. "It's not quite a nest. Should I bring more?"

My toes curl in the carpet. "It will do just fine."

He pats the mattress, and hesitantly, I let the towels fall to the ground and crawl inside. A heated blanket warms my hands and knees as I move to the far side and poke at the pillows before I curl against them. When Emil slides in on the other side and pulls the blankets up, I peer over my shoulder at him and realize he didn't save a pillow for himself.

Uncertain, I try to choose one to give back, but they all form to a different part of my body, and returning one throws everything else out of balance. I glance back at him. "Do you need a pillow?"

"I'll make do." He ducks under the blankets, and a moment later, a cold arm curls around my hips. I yelp with surprise, then relax as he nuzzles against my side with a chilly sigh of contentment. Frost creeps into my skin, overriding the burns Domnall left inside.

With a smile, I tug one of the pillows over my head and snuggle down.

WHAT A DEMON WANTS

I barge into HelloHell Delivery at noon on the dot.

Imp heads pop up from around their cubicles, eyes wide before they disappear once more. The entire place smells like baby powder and coconut body oil with stripper clothes hanging from free standing racks against the back walls. Chittering fills the room as I stride for my cousin's office at the back, and for a second, I catch the flash of Iris's rainbow head peeking up at me before she goes back into hiding.

As I near the frosted glass doors, with Julian's name printed across the front, I notice a new desk set off to the side. Tiny, it barely allows for a chair to scoot under it, and the phone on its wooden surface takes up half the space. A planner fills the rest.

From behind it, Philip smiles at me. He's

Julian's right-hand man, or as close as my cousin gets to one.

Today, he swapped out his usual black t-shirt and tight jeans for a looser pair of slacks and a dress shirt, aiming for a more professional flare. With his baby face, he looks like a teenager on his way to his first school dance.

I pause next to his desk and smile back at him. "Moving up in the world, I see."

He leans forward, batting his eyelashes at me. "I'm still on the menu if you're interested."

I snort. "What would you do if I actually said yes?"

"Strip." At my horrified expression, he shrugs and leans back. "You wouldn't turn me to dust, and sex with your kind is hot. I can spare some energy."

"You shouldn't take that kind of risk. You've worked for Julian long enough that you've made back your contract." My hands move to my hips. "And how do you know I wouldn't drain you dry?"

"You're not that kind of demon." His gaze flicks to the left, and I twist in time to catch Kelly as he disappears into his cubicle. When I turn back, Philip runs possessive hands over the edges of his tiny desk. "And I like this work. I'm good at it."

"Well, congratulations on the upgrade." I glance

at the office door, where yellow light shines through. "Is he free?"

"Yes." He reaches for the phone, then pauses and the playfulness leaves his expression. Voice low, he whispers, "I didn't tell him you'd be in today or that you're interested in buying out any contracts."

Surprise rushes through me. I was stupid enough to let my interest slip yesterday in front of him, why wouldn't he give his boss the advantage? If Julian knew I *wanted* the imps permanently, he'd put their price through the roof.

Slowly, I nod. This favor won't go unpaid.

Philip lifts the phone and presses a button. A quiet buzz comes from inside the office, followed by the creak of a chair, and the buzzing stops.

Voice chipper, Philip announces, "Ms. Adeline Pond to see you, sir."

Whoa, the guy really pushes that secretary vibe.

"Yes, I'll see her in." He hangs up and stands to round the desk, his hand out. "If you will follow me?"

I keep the smile off my face as he leads me the one step to the office door.

He opens it and extends his arm inside. "Would you care for a water?"

"No, thank you." I pass him and walk into the office.

Julian sits behind his cherry oak desk, his white curls showing a hint of pink at the tips. He must be really busy lately. He never lets his color show. Shadows rest under his blue eyes, and the pink in his cheeks holds a powdery quality that shouts of makeup.

I frown as I walk over to him, concern pushing aside my original purpose. "Hey, you doing okay? You're looking a little dim."

He sniffs delicately. "Well, aren't you rude, first thing in the morning?"

"Cassandra hasn't come back, has she?" After evil Cassandra almost devoured him, any sign of ill-health on his part makes me worry.

"No, darling, I'm just working too much and haven't been able to find myself some nice, human plaything to give me an extra boost."

Relief dispels the concern. Though he needs to find time to feed, I keep my commentary to myself. I'm the last succubi who can pass judgement in that area.

His bookshelf catches my attention, and I go to investigate the titles as the Quest the Librarian sent me on flashes back to the front of my mind. But when I skim the titles, they all look pretty basic, porn magazines mixed in with business journals.

I peer over my shoulder. "Have you borrowed any books from the library?"

One white eyebrow lifts. "Who has time for that, darling?"

"People who want to educate themselves?" Abandoning the bookshelf, I plop into one of the padded seats across from him.

His lip curls in distaste before he demands, "What do you want?"

When I came here, I expected him to already know the reason. Now that I hold the advantage, I'm not sure how to play into it. Settling into the padded seat, I cross my legs, mind whirling. "It's about the imps—"

His pointed finger cuts me off. "You can't return them. You're under contract. And you've ruined them for my business."

Startled, I blink at him. "But I—"

He slashes a hand through the air. "No. I don't care that one of them refuses to take form. You're stuck with them." He pushes to his feet with a squeak. "In fact, you need to figure out somewhere else for them to stay. They're infecting my other imps."

"What's that supposed to mean?" I leap to my feet. "And their room and board *here* is part of our contract!"

"Let me show you." He strides for the door, his vinyl red short-shorts shaking angrily. When we reach the outer office, he claps loudly, and imps pop up from around the room, vibrating with alertness. He points to one on the left. "There, do you see?"

I follow the line of his arm to an attractive man with lean muscles and tan skin. His thick, dark hair forms perfect waves, and his features remind me of a famous porn star.

Bewildered, I glance at Julian. "What am I supposed to be seeing?"

His hands flap in agitation. "The beard, darling! The *beard*!"

I squint and make out a thin, dark shadow along the imp's jawline. "What about it?"

"HelloHell Delivery is a clean-cut service!" He spins to the right and points to another imp. "And *that*! How am I supposed to market *that*?"

This imp sports a fashionable purple streak in her sleek, black hair. "I really don't see the problem here."

"*Your* imps are giving *my* imps bad ideas about

what's acceptable." He spins and wags a finger at me. "This is *your* responsibility."

The corners of my lips twitch. "*My* imps?"

"Yes, *your* imps." He points to my group of five, who stand out among the rest of the stripper quality imps. "You need to *do* something about this before it becomes an epidemic and my business is *ruined*."

I fold my hands behind my back. "You agreed to pay for their room and board, and delivery to and from the bakery. You're contracted. Not much I can do about that." I keep the smile off my face. "Unless you want to renegotiate?"

His eyes narrow into thin slits. "What do you want?"

"It's not about what *I* want, dear cousin." With one hand on his shoulder, I gesture back to the office. "It's all about what *you* want."

∽

An hour later, I leave Julian's office with a new contract already filed at the demons' clerk's office. Excitement and nervousness rattle through my bones. I have a week to find my imps a new place to live, then they'll be *mine*. The savings on renting them will be outweighed by having to pay for their room and board, though. Which means I need to find someplace cheap.

For a second, the idea of hiding them in my room pops into my head, but I shake it away. The guys would never let that happen. Or, would they? I shake my head again. No, they definitely wouldn't.

I check my watch. Tally agreed to come in for the morning baking, which means I have a few hours before I need to be at the store.

Waffling on what to do, I climb into my car and pull out onto the main street.

Finding a new place for my imps seems like the most important task right now. But a flash of light in a nearby doorway reminds me I need to start looking for this stupid book the hag wants back so much. Though, how I'm supposed to find it, I have no idea.

My old apartment is only a couple blocks away. If I remember right, Julian rented it out to a trio of our cousins. Maybe I should swing by there. But will they even be awake yet? With how we feed, most succubi and incubi keep a nocturnal schedule.

I don't have enough time to drive out to Landon's and search his house, and the idea of being alone with him still makes me nervous. As my mentor, I can't avoid him forever, but a couple more days can't hurt, right? Besides, I'll have to clean the place before I can search it, which will take all day. I don't even want to consider the mountain of water bottles and delivery boxes that must fill his house by now. When I eventually go, I'm taking another house cleaning brochure with me.

Unsure what to do, I find myself driving down the street that leads back to the house. This morning, I was lucky that Emil set an alarm for me when he left for work. I didn't even feel the ice demon leave, and Tac refused to come near me, so no wake up snuggle to jog me into awareness.

I lift my arm to sniff it. Does Domnall's scent still cling to me?

All I smell is bath soap and Emil, but maybe the giant cat monster senses some of Domnall's energy still floating around inside me. I thought I puked it all out, but my stomach rolls every so often with unease. I want to scrub my insides, flood out all the energy that lingers, and replace it with fresh, new energy. Unfortunately, that would mean draining myself dry. Hard to do after the semi-date with Kellen and a cuddly night with Emil.

Well, not that hard. I could burn it off with a couple hyper-speed laps around the city. But I'd need a ready source of fresh energy immediately after. Then, I'd have to explain to the guys why I felt the need to drain myself.

Feeding off a human to replenish my supply is a solid *no*. While they're easy meals, I don't want to hurt them. They're so weak and easy to damage. The idea adds a new, unwanted layer of unease to my stomach.

Nope. Not happening.

When I pull into the driveway, I'm surprised to find Kellen's black luxury car there. Usually he parks it in the side garage, along with Tobias's and Emil's cars. Did he leave early for the club and come back for some reason?

Climbing out, I head into the house, ears perked for noise. The old house creaks as it shifts under the weight of summer, and the air conditioner quietly hums. I kick off my bright blue clogs and walk farther inside. From the living room, I can see most of the empty kitchen.

Curious, I eye the staircase on to the right of the fireplace that leads up to Tobias's and Kellen's rooms. But the memory of how my date with Kellen ended steers my feet to the left staircase and up to my room in the attic. I'm still not happy with the way he dismissed me after claiming me as his woman.

At my doorway, my steps slow. The scent of ozone and lightning lingers at the threshold, as if Kellen stood in the doorway for some time. It's faint enough that it happened hours ago, possibly while I was sleeping down in Emil's room. How did I miss it this morning when I got ready for work? Had Kellen come to find me when he got home this morning?

My wings shift against my spine with uncertainty. We never really talked about what being *his woman* meant. Should I not have let him make that kind of claim? Could I be his woman and still be with Emil and Tobias? Kellen's well aware of my current contract with his roommates, but demons are a jealous, greedy race.

I venture into my room and find my laptop, then curl into the corner of my floral-patterned couch. Someday, I'm going to drag it downstairs to stake my claim on the spot in front of the fireplace. But not until *after* Kellen and I replace Tobais's favorite chair, which lays in two pieces, shoved against the wall downstairs.

Yet another thing to take care of at some point. The list keeps getting longer. With a heavy sigh, I flip open the laptop and pull up a search for local apartments.

Not a Slum Lord

"Watcha doin?"

I jump at the question and twist to see the open doorway. Apartment listings still fill my vision, the initial price tag giving my heart serious issues. My one bedroom didn't cost this much when I moved in. What happened to the housing market?

Blinking to clear my eyes, I find Kellen lounging against the door frame, arms folded over his muscular chest and one ankle hooked behind the other. He looks like he's been there a while, watching me cringe in horror.

With a small frown for the lightning demon, I slouch down in the couch until he disappears from view. "None of your business."

He blows out a loud breath. "So, you *are* mad at me."

I glare at the latest listing, a three bedroom for twenty-five hundred a month. "Don't know what you're talking about."

"I'm sorry about our date last night. That's not how I wanted it to end." His soft apology comes with the hint of summer rain, and I close my laptop before I peek at him over the back of the couch. One side of his mouth kicks up. "I came to talk to you last night, but you were hiding from me."

"I wasn't hiding." I duck back out of view. "Emil just asked me to stay with him last night."

His feet shuffle against the hardwood. "Is that a new thing you're doing?"

I pop back up to make sure he didn't cross my threshold. Hands on either side of the door frame, his toes nudge at the invisible line that marks my territory while he leans as far into my room as possible without technically entering.

My eyes narrow at the not-quite-intrusion. "It was a first. Might not be a last."

"Was there snuggling involved?" Interest fills his voice, and his muscles strain as he leans farther in. "How do I get to participate next time?"

Rising onto my knees, I fold my arms over the back of the couch. "Don't be a dick, for one."

"Emil wasn't being a dick?" His eyebrows shoot

up in surprise, then swoop back down. "Wait. You just called me a dick, didn't you?"

Ignoring that, I ask, "Who's Domnall?"

His face hardens. "Stay away from him, Adie."

Too late. I bite back the words. For Slater's protection, Kellen can never know what happened yesterday. I circle around to try a different tactic to get Kellen to talk about him. "Is he dangerous?"

"He's a demon."

My lips thin with annoyance at his evasiveness. "So am I."

"He's a bigger demon." He extends a hand. "Can I come in?"

"No."

"Please?"

Instead, I climb over the top of the couch, walk to the door, and stop just out of his reach. "What if I run into him again? Don't you think I should know who I'm dealing with?"

The muscle in his jaw clenches. "If you see him, you hyper-speed as far away as you can get. Bad things happen when he's near."

So, I noticed. Did he attack me to spite Kellen? Will he do it again? Or was he just in desperate need of an energy drain last night?

I should send out a warning to my local cousins

to stay away from him, just in case. While they're all more powerful than I am, and can probably handle that kind of energy dump better, it's a nasty way to be used and not something any of them deserve.

Well, maybe Cassandra. But she left town.

Kellen's face softens. "Don't worry. He usually stays out of my side of town. He came last night to ask permission to hunt in my territory. He should be back on the west side now."

Alarmed now, I venture closer. "What was he hunting? Was it a succubi or incubi?"

His brows furrow together. "Why would you think that?"

My shoulders stiffen. "No reason."

His expression clears. "Oh, is it because he offered to buy you out? I'm sorry I made it sound like you're just a contract last night. I don't want Domnall more interested in you by letting him know we're involved."

Pleasure makes my toes curl. "We're involved?"

"Well, you're my woman, aren't you?" Reaching out, his fingertips stop an inch away from my arm and electricity jumps the space to nip at me. "Come closer."

I sway toward him, then immediately bounce

back out of reach as I remember my earlier concern. "I think we need to talk first."

"I think you think too much."

Affronted, I rise onto my toes. "I think you want to sleep alone from now on."

"That's fine, I guess. I'm not really interested in sleeping when you're around." He waggles his fingers at me. "Now, come here so we can not-sleep."

"You're impossible."

He skims a hand down his chest. "I'm entirely possible."

I perk up with sudden interest. "Hey, you own a bunch of property, right?"

With a heartfelt sigh, he leans back against the doorframe. "Why do I feel like this just got that much farther from sexy time?"

"Because it did." I spin and go back to the couch, lean over the back, and grab my laptop. "I've just spent the last fifty minutes looking at apartment listings, and it's all horrible."

The air crackles with sudden electricity, thunder rumbling through the floor. "You're moving out?"

"No." Refusing to be intimidated, I march back to stand in front of him. "But I need to find a place for my imps."

The tension eases from the room. "I thought your cousin housed them."

"Not for much longer." I bounce on my toes with excitement. "They'll be mine, fully contracted, next week."

A frown tugs at the corners of his mouth. "But you're broke, or close enough to it."

"Well"—I sidle closer—"I won't be paying for their rental anymore, so I'll put that toward a safe place for them."

His eyes narrow. "How much are you looking to spend?"

Currently, I pay one-seventy-five a week for each of them, but I may have to buy furniture. Plus, I'll have to compensate for food from now on, and picking them up and dropping them off...

I bite my lip. "Eighteen hundred?"

"I can get you a two bedroom for that." He grabs my waist. "Now that business is out of the way—"

I throw a hand up. "I need at least a three bedroom."

He tugs me closer to the threshold. "Not possible in this market."

I plant my palms against his chest to maintain my distance. "There's five of them, Kellen."

"Get them bunk beds."

"And I need money to feed them."

"Feed them at the bakery." Giving up on closing the distance between us, he takes a step back and drags me out of my room.

"You're being an asshole again."

He bares his teeth in aggravation. "You're trying to use my desire for you to your advantage."

"How's it working?"

He growls, a low rumble of thunder in his chest. "Not well."

"Kellen, I'm serious here. I need a place for them to live." My fingers flex against his hard pecs. "Don't you have anywhere that's super cheap? Where no one will give the little gray one a second glance?"

"I'm not a slum lord, Adie." Sparks nip at my skin in reprimand.

"Nothing?" I unlock my arm enough to let him pull me two inches closer before I stiffen my muscles once more. "You really don't have *anything* available?"

Uncertainty flickers across his face. "Well..."

"Yes?" I bounce on my toes in excitement. When his gaze drops to my boobs, I bounce a couple more times for good measure. But when he stays silent, I press, "You thought of something?"

"There's a house. Six bedroom." His hands slide up to my ribcage. "But it's complete shit. I've been meaning to clean it up, but..."

"I'll take it!" I fling my arms around his neck. "Thank you!"

His arms circle my body. "You might want to look at it before you agree."

"Can we go now?" I kiss his cheek and feel the curve of a smile against my lips. "Pretty please?"

"Fine." Reluctant, he releases me and steps back. "But don't say I didn't warn you."

∽

When I follow Kellen down the twisting alleys, I begin to get suspicious. It feels too much like the path to Tally's rundown mansion. And when he parks two houses down from hers, trepidation sets in.

Parking my car next to Kellen's, I climb and carefully make my way across the broken driveway to join him. "This place is a complete dump."

With boarded up windows and a rotted, sagging porch, the narrow, three-story house glares out over the street. Moss covers the roof, and vines climb up to cover the garage. The light fixture next to the door hangs by the wires and swings gently.

I turn back to Kellen, eyes wide. "Are you *sure* you're not a slumlord?"

"I told you it was bad." He swings the keys around his finger. "Want to go check out one of the two-bedroom apartments?"

"We should at least look inside first." Uncertainty makes my voice small. "Show me around."

He catches the keys in his hand. "I'd rather not."

I completely agree. The entire place gives off a giant *go away* vibe that makes my feet want to head back to the car. It pushes at me with a sense of urgency I find hard to resist. But my imps need a home, and unless I want to stack them into a tiny apartment, this is my only option.

Shoulders squared, I push the feeling aside.

"We're here. Stop being a baby." Latching onto his arm, I tug him toward the broken steps up to the porch.

"Careful of the hole," he says as we reach the top.

A giant, black expanse of broken boards bars our way, and I peer down into it, surprised not to see dead grass and dirt beneath. Instead, dark shadows swath the opening and make it impossible to see the bottom. "Where does this end?"

"Never ventured down to find out." He kicks a loose board into the hole, and we wait with our breaths held. Silence stretches out, and my lungs begin to burn from lack of oxygen.

I release my pent-up breath. "Is it some kind of portal or something?"

He shrugs.

"Why would you leave it exposed like this?"

"A cult used to live here. Lots of people died. No one wanted to rent it, so why dump money into repairs?"

I stare at him in disbelief. "Because anyone who ventures up here could get hurt?"

"There's a no trespassing sign." He crooks a thumb to a small, rectangle sign that hangs from one nail next to the stairs. "Demons know not to come here, and humans who break the law deserve what they get."

"How do demons know not to come here?"

He glances at me in surprise. "Don't you feel it?"

"Feel what?" I rub my arms. The longer we stand here, the more I want to leave.

"You're kidding, right?" When I stare at him

blankly, he shakes his head. "That sense that's telling you to not come here?"

My eyes dart around the porch. Shadows hug every corner, despite the midday sun, and cobwebs fill the open rafters. "Yeah, the place is creepy."

"No, I mean that literal push for you to go away." He catches my hands and pulls them away from my arms. "There's a spell to tell people to go away."

"Oh." My fingers curl against my tingly palms. "Is that what this is?" My nose itches, and I rub it against my shoulder. "I don't have a lot of experience with human magic." I shake his hands off and rub my face. "Is it always this annoying?"

"This one's lost focus." He rolls his shoulders. "Still want to go inside?"

"Yeah, let's get this over with." We hug the railing to circle the gaping hole and edge back to the door. Like Tally's house, an ugly, lion's head knocker sits front and center, its ruby eyes dull.

I poke at its wrinkled snout. "What's up with these?"

"No idea. Maybe they're supposed to scare away evil spirits?" He swings the keys around his finger again. "Last chance to turn back."

"Why does this feel like a bad horror movie?" I

run a hand through my hair, thankful I'm not a blond or I'd be in real trouble.

He arches one fiery eyebrow. "Because the house is obviously haunted, and you want to go in anyway?"

I scoff at him. "Stop trying to scare me off. As long as the roof doesn't leak and the electricity works, I'm renting this place."

"Don't say I didn't warn you." He shoves the key into the lock and pushes the door open.

Like Tally's house, marble covers the floor, though an inch of dust and dirt obscures its beauty. I step over the threshold and peer up at the vaulted ceiling. A sheet-covered chandelier hangs overhead, probably crystal and in need of a good polish, but promising.

I glance over my shoulder at Kellen, who hovers at the entrance. "This isn't so bad."

He folds his arms over his chest. "You say that now, but you've only seen the foyer."

Dirt sifts under the soles of my sneakers, making the floor slippery. "Which way is the kitchen?"

"That's always where you look first, isn't it?"

"The kitchen is the heart of the home!" I call back as I venture past the curved staircase. When silence follows, I turn back to find Kellen still on the porch. My hands move to my hips. "What are you waiting for? You're here to give me a tour."

"Adie, maybe you should come back out here." He reaches out a hand, fingers extended, and the front door slams shut on him.

Darkness blacks out my vision, then sharp nails scrape against the walls, followed by an eerie, hollow voice. "What new treat has ventured into our home?"

Oh, fuck. Kellen was serious. This place is *actually* haunted.

And I'm trapped inside.

Monster Hunt

My phone rings, cutting off the hissing whispers of doom. Whipping it out of my back pocket, the bright glow of the screen floods the hallway.

I swipe the answer button and press it against my ear. "Why didn't you *tell* me this place was haunted?"

Kellen's voice comes across way too calm. "I *did*. It's not my fault you're so completely oblivious."

"You could have tried harder! I'm on my way back out." Hanging up, I use the phone's light, I spin in a tight circle before I figure out which direction leads back to the entrance.

The skitter of claws rush past me, followed by the dry slither of scales through dust. This haunter likes to rely heavily on the creepy crawly fear.

When I grab the door handle and twist, it won't budge. What that...?

Spindling out a line of power, I add strength and give it a hard twist. The knob comes off in my hand, but the door stays firmly shut.

Frustrated, I kick the damn thing. "I don't have time for this shit!"

In my hand, my phone rings.

I snap it back to my ear. "You *knew* this would happen."

"You wanted someplace cheap where your imps didn't have to bunk together," Kellen reminds me. "I offered another solution *multiple* times."

"Why haven't you had this place exorcised?" Something with more than eight legs drops onto my shoulder, and I swat it away.

"You think I keep a coven of witches on speed dial or something?"

Yes. I bite my tongue before the word escapes. Kellen owns Tally's men in some way, but I'm not sure I'm supposed to know about Slater and Xander's iffy skills.

I rest my forehead against the door. "Just tell me how to get out of here."

"Once it's triggered, you have to go all the way to the basement and defeat the nightmare."

"This really is a fucking horror movie." I pound my head against the door. *Thump, thump, thump.* An answering thud comes from the stairs, uneven as if the person hobbles on a stump for one leg. Sighing, I ask, "How do I defeat the nightmare?"

"Sunlight."

A wicked cackle fills the room, and I cover one ear. "In the basement?"

"There's a mirror system you have to rig up. Shouldn't take you more than an hour."

"Fuck my life."

"Take your time and check out the rest of the house before you go downstairs," he suggests. "See if you like the place."

"Yeah, I guess." I straighten and turn back toward the dark house. "How's the roof on this place?"

"Solid."

I start toward the stairs. "And the bedrooms?"

"They're decent size. One master and five standard."

The first step creaks ominously under my foot, but the wood feels solid enough. Hard to say if it's construction or part of the haunt. Just to be safe, I put the phone on speaker and angle the flashlight down to see each step before I put my weight on it.

"How many bathrooms?"

"Two upstairs and a powder room on the ground floor."

"Seriously? In a house this size?" A shadow flitters past. It holds the shape of wings and claws designed for rending flesh. "Hey, how solid is this nightmare? Should I be worried?"

"Naw, it's all show." A quiet click sounds, and music floods through the phone before it cuts off.

A scowl twists my lips. "Are you sitting in your car?"

"What, you want me to hang out next to the potentially bottomless hole while I wait?"

"No, I guess not." I huff out a breath. "You can go to work if you want. You don't need to wait."

"Well, aren't you considerate," he purrs.

"Maybe you don't want to be around when I get out of this," I suggest as another bug falls on me. This one tangles in my hair, tiny legs tickling my scalp before I pick it out and toss it over the rail. "I'm not going to be in a good mood once I escape."

He gives an appreciative laugh. "Now that you mention it, I *do* have a meeting I should prepare for."

"Yes, run away now."

"You sure?" His engine rumbles to life. "It's your

suggestion, so you can't be mad at me later for leaving."

"I'll be rushing to work as soon as I'm out of this, so there's no reason for you to stay." I reach the landing and venture to the first door. Patting the wall, I find the light switch and flip it. Unsurprisingly, nothing happens. When I wave my phone's flashlight around, it looks like a standard box with closet and windows. "Hey, there's no drapes."

"I think the cult used them to swaddle their animal sacrifices or something." Quiet road noise sounds in the background as Kellen drives away. "I'll replace them if you really rent the house."

The next four rooms on this level look the same, and a large linen closet gives plenty of storage. "It actually looks pretty nice." A soda can skitters away from the toe of my shoe. "Aside from the trash."

"You'll have some work to do."

I venture up to the third floor. The stairs open out into a rec room, with the master bedroom taking up the remainder of the level. Which imp will take this one? I haven't noticed any specific one seeming to take the lead in their group.

As I glance around the large space, I tap my phone against my hand in consideration. "I'll pay fifteen hundred for this place, and not a penny more."

"The price is eighteen hundred," he reminds me.

"It's haunted and needs too much work. As it is, it's a money drain on you just to pay the property taxes." I turn back to head downstairs. "You're lucky I'm willing to go as high as fifteen hundred. Do you know how much an exorcism will cost? If I can even find a witch?"

"Fine." Sharp edges fill his voice. No demon likes to be out bargained, but he must realize this is likely the only way he'll get this house to make a profit again.

"I want to see that contract on the kitchen counter tonight when I get home."

"You think I just have contracts laying around?" he demands. "I'm a busy man."

"A busy man who doesn't really have a meeting right now," I counter. "Contract tonight, or the deal's off."

"Fine," he snaps. "I'm not overly fond of you right now."

"Then we're even." Something furry brushes against my arm, and my skin crawls. "I'm not enjoying this haunt at all."

Annoyance still fills his voice when he adds, "I still want to cuddle tonight."

"We'll see. Bye now." I hang up after his gruff response and pull up my text messages.

Adie: Hey, Tally, can you have Xander and Reese come to the bakery tonight?

I tour the ground floor while I wait for her to respond. The family room leads into a dining room, which then leads into a decent-sized kitchen. It's hard to tell in the dark, but it looks like the appliances are at least functional, although nowhere near as nice as the set at my house.

Finally, my phone beeps with a new message.

Tally: May I ask why?

My fingers fly over the digital keyboard.

Adie: I have a proposition for them.

Adie: It will earn them some extra cash.

I stare at the screen for a solid minute before her reply comes back.

Tally: Okay.

If the long pause is anything to go by, she's hesitant. Is she afraid I'll betray her secret, even after I promised not to? While that hurts, I also can't fault her for it. We haven't really known each other long. Our friendship is still new enough to leave room for surprises.

Lots of surprises.

I find the door to the basement behind the stairs. When I open it, I'm surprised to find the light works. Must be part of the haunting, since none of the other switches I flipped got the electricity flowing.

The bare lightbulb swings from a cord, with no visible reason why except that it throws eerie shadows over the steep staircase, making the footing treacherous. I stare down at the open-backed steps. Perfect for creepy monsters to reach through and grab at ankles.

Humans would be foolhardy to venture down there.

My wings slip from my back, feathers stretching, and I vault over the rail. Shadows roil below, tentacles waiting to grasp at the unwary. Flapping, I gain enough lift to make it to the half window that peeks above ground. Not big enough to create an exit, but large enough to give hope of escape. Years of built up grime cover the glass and block out the sun.

I shove it open, old paint and age making it stick in the frame. A narrow beam of light shoots inside. Which makes zero sense. The narrow street outside doesn't allow for a lot of natural light, and the position of this window puts it on the east side, far away from where the sun now sits in the sky. Sunlight shouldn't be an option at all right now, and yet it creates a solid laser beam. Where it touches, the rolling mass lets out a shriek as it slithers away.

Why does it feel like I'm dealing with a lot of shrieking masses of tentacle monsters lately? This better not devolve into one of those weird, animated porn movies.

Clinging to the side of the wall, I search the ground for the mirrors Kellen spoke of. The whole thing reminds me of one of Landon's video games, only with a lot less battle. I spot a round disk peeking out from under the stairs, and more round disks hidden throughout the basement. If it's like a video game, they'll be perfectly positioned. All I'll have to do is shift one into the beam of light, and the rest will flood the room with sunbeams, obliterating the nightmare.

With a deep breath, I dive for the staircase, grab the mirror, and bounce up into the air again before any of the tentacles grab ahold of me. The mirror's sharp edges cut into my palms as I gauge the floor for the best angle to place it. I land in the narrow beam of light. Shadows writhe at the edges, and a loud, angry rumble fills the basement.

The evil voice from earlier floods the room. "You will not escape."

"Oh, shut it," I snap as I place the mirror into the sunbeam. I angle it to the first mirror I find, attached to the rafters.

It flares to life, creating a zigzag of light that floods the basement. Which also makes zero sense. The angles are all wrong. But nevertheless, the nightmare shrieks and flails as it finds itself without a corner to hide in.

"You will not defeat me!" it howls, and a cloud of black rushes toward me.

I turn the mirror, and like a lightsaber, it cuts the monster in two, turning it to black sand.

The sunlight vanishes, dropping me back into momentary darkness before the overhead lights flick on. My wings snap against my spine as I drag the mirror back to its place behind the stairs.

Stupidest haunting ever. The cult that lived here had no imagination.

I just hope Tally's guys will be able to cleanse the place. I'd hate for the imps to have to live in this. That would get annoying fast.

With the lights back on, I make a fast retreat before the house resets itself and forces me to defeat the nightmare again.

My old sedan waits by itself in the driveway, like nothing crazy just happened, and I climb inside. Heat hugs me, and I turn on the engine to get the air conditioner going.

After a moment, I pull my phone back out and shoot Kellen a text.

Adie: Escaped. No epic battle.

He sends back a sad face, which pulls a surprised laugh from me, and I tuck the phone next to the emergency break before backing out of the driveway.

In retrospect, today hasn't been *too* bad. I got my imps from Julian, found them an inexpensive place to live, and I'll only be half an hour late to work.

Not bad at all.

(UN)HURRIED

As soon as I walk through the side door at the bakery, I realize I made a mistake. But I'm halfway across the threshold when the spark of a portal alerts me to the danger. I try to backtrack, but the hag catches me, her talons cutting into my forearm as she yanks me through.

I stumble and almost trip over her diminutive form before I catch myself. "What the fuck?"

"You are not taking your Quest seriously," she hisses as she releases me.

"It hasn't even been a day!" I rub the blood from my skin, annoyed at expending energy to heal the damage.

Her head tilts up in an unnatural angle as she glares at me through the folds of her eyelids. "You seem to think this is some kind of game that you can take your time on."

I glance around at the hall of doorways. It's becoming far too familiar. "I'm taking it seriously. I already searched one place."

"Because it was convenient to you at the time."

Surprised, I turn back to her. "Are you watching me?"

He black tongue flicks out. "Always."

"That's a little creepy." When she remains silent, I fold my hands behind my back. "I'll keep looking."

"Do it faster."

"What's so important about this book?" Maybe if she tells me more about it, I can figure out which cousin might have checked it out.

"The safety of the city relies on it being found."

That snaps me to attention. "What do you mean?"

"Exactly what I said. Now, go find it." And with that, she shoves me back through the doorway.

I land with a heavy thud against the alley wall, disoriented by the fast change in scenery. Doorways are no longer my friend. Why do they exist *everywhere*?

Straightening, I eye the frame for any telltale sparks before venturing into Boo's Boutique Bakery. Relief washes through me when I make it inside without another incident.

What could the Librarian have meant by a book saving the city? Can books do that? And what did the city need to be saved from? Or did she just say that to make me search harder?

The comforting scent of butter and sugar pulls me toward the kitchen and the soft chitter of voices. The air feels less hollow already, the drain of happy emotions caused by Domnall's attack already on the mend.

Tally must have had one of the guys in early today to cleanse the space of negativity. Kind of wish I was here for that. I've never seen a cleansing.

As I walk into the kitchen, imps glance up from their tasks, and happy grins spread across their faces.

Kelly drops his measuring cup full of flour and wraps his burly arms around me. "Master, thank you."

"Hey, now, none of that." Surprised, I wiggle out of his embrace, only to have Iris surround me in a cloud of rainbow.

"Master, thank you," she coos softly.

"Stop!" I get an arm free, and Martha arrives to smother me against her motherly bosom.

The smell of espresso clings to her as she pats the back of my head. "Master, thank you."

"Come on, guys, I don't want you to—"

Reed thin arms wrap around my waist, and Jesse chitters a heartfelt, "Master, thank you."

Iris swoops back in on the hug, and Kelly wraps his large arms around all of us, squishing us together.

Through a gap in their bodies, I spot Tally as she walks through the swinging door. Her mahogany eyes widen, then she claps softly. "Oh, congratulations, Adie. The imps already told me."

Hearing my name, Perry runs into the kitchen and throws himself into the group hug with a delighted, "Master, thank you."

"Okay, that's enough." Using my elbows, I extricate myself from the baby powder club and turn to point at them. "None of this 'master' stuff. You're not property."

"But Adie is now first, so she is master." Iris sweeps toward me, her arms open, and I dart away to put the kitchen island between us.

I throw my hands up to stop her. "I'm not okay with that title. I don't *own* you guys."

"But you own our contracts," Kelly rumbles.

Iris nods. "You sheltered us from The Red Death."

The Red What? Was she talking about cousin Cassandra?

Martha clasps her hands in front of her soft breasts. "You hid us from The Destroyer."

Who the What?

"You bargained for our contracts so we can choose our forms without hindrance." Perry stares at me, his heavy-lidded gaze filled with open worship.

"Adeline Boo Pond is The Protector of Imps," Jesse pipes up in a high-pitched voice.

"Now, wait just a minute." That last statement had the ring of naming to it. "Let's not get carried away here."

Somewhere in the library, there's a thin book carving my history onto the pages, and no way do I want to be known as the Protector of Imps.

"It is done," the little group announces.

A slender hand settles on my shoulder, and Tally's clay scent envelopes me. "It is a great honor to be named so young."

I twist to stare at her in disbelief. "Are you serious?"

She nods solemnly.

"But I don't want that name," I hiss, quiet enough that the imps can't hear.

"We do not choose what we will be named. Embrace it with pride." She turns to the imps and claps once more. "Now, back to work! There's no one up front serving customers!"

They disperse in a rush, trailing soft touches across my arms as they move back to their assignments.

Tally turns to Martha. "Will you please run the cash register while I meet with Adie?"

"Of course!" Martha pulls the hairnet from her head and fluffs her short bob before she pushes through the swinging doors.

Next, Tally turns to Kelly. "Please make sure the next batch of lemon cakes get into the oven. The sunflowers are popular with the before dinner rush."

"Yes, ma'am." The large, biker imp lifts his measuring cup once more and carefully weighs out the flour.

I blink at Tally in surprise. "You're doing really well at lead today."

She leans in close, her expression conspiratorial. "I ate a manager's dream. It took me a couple nights to find the right one. Do you know how many unprofessional people are put in charge of others?"

"Way too many."

She nods, then grabs my arm. "Let us go to the office to speak."

"You know, I was thinking we should convert part of the upstairs to be a real office and break room." I follow her down the hall toward the large pantry. "There's not a lot stored up there."

She glances back at me, her brows furrowed. "I thought you disliked the stairway?"

"It turns out it was an unnecessary avoidance." If the Librarian can grab me at any doorway, there's no need to hide from the attic.

"Then, it is a good plan." She pushes open the pantry door and waits for me to enter first before crowding inside to shut it. "Now, please explain why you need to speak to Xander and Reese."

Tension lines the corners of her mouth and eyes, and I grip her arms. "Tally, don't worry. I told you I'd protect them, and I will. That's not what this is about."

Some of the tension eases from her muscles. "They did not like being told to stay away today."

"Then, you should let them know they can come back. This is a safe space for them." I drop my arms to my side and lean a hip against the desk wedged against one wall. "You said you might know someone who could cleanse the negativity from the shop. And since it seems to be gone, I'm guessing you already had that done?"

She gives a tight nod.

I rub my palms together. "So, as you heard, I bought the contracts for the imps."

She nods again, more relaxed this time, though uncertainty still fills her expression.

"Well, I think I found them a house, but it has some issues I'm hoping Xander or Reese might be able to help with." Nervous sweat breaks out along my sides. I didn't want to know more about these witches than I needed to, but circumstances changed. "It's actually located a couple houses down from yours."

Her eyes widen. "Not the haunted one?"

My shoulders hunch. Even she knew it was really haunted? "Yeah, that one."

"Is there not another option?"

"Not one I'm happy with. My budget is pretty limited on this." I straighten. "I'd be willing to pay them, though I have no idea what the going rate is for exorcisms. I don't even know how to look that kind of thing up."

"There's a website." She pulls out her phone and rolls the pink case between her fingers in thought.

After a moment, she admits, "They're not that good."

"Yeah, I figured that out when Xander tried to banish Domnall," I say drily. "But the haunt isn't that strong. I don't think it will take much effort to dispel."

"They can at least take a look?"

"I'd appreciate it." Relief sweeps through me.

If she refused, I had no idea who to turn to next. Though knowing there's a website helps. Maybe witches aren't as reclusive as they used to be? Especially since the higher ups made it forbidden to hunt them?

As she shoots off a couple text messages, I remember the giant hole in the porch and the sagging roof. Those won't disappear after the house is cleared of bad magic. "Do you think Jax might be up for doing some wood work, too? The porch is pretty bad."

Now, she relaxes completely and grins. "Yes, he is very good with his hands and will appreciate the opportunity."

"Great! Just let me know when they can meet with me to take a look at the house."

She nods, sends off another message, then catches me up to speed with where the bakery is at so far today. Eating the manager's dreams really did give her a leg up on this kind of thing. Confidence fills her voice as she talks about sell rates and makes suggestions on rotating flavors for the week.

If I'm not careful, she'll know the bakery better than I do.

～

At six o'clock, Tobias arrives at the bakery. I spot his dark head over the line of after work customers and ask Martha to start a peppermint tea for him to be ready by the time he reaches the register.

My heart picks up speed the closer he gets. It feels like I haven't seen Tobias in a while, even though he grumped at me only yesterday. Which reminds me, Kellen and I still need to replace his favorite chair. I peek at him, now third in line, and his dark gaze catches mine.

He doesn't seem unhappy. Hopefully, he didn't come here to yell at me again.

Breaking the chair was Kellen's fault, anyway. He should be the one who gets yelled at.

Delicious ozone fills my nose as the elderly lady in front of me takes her blue rose cupcake and Tobias replaces her in line.

Martha passes me his tea, and I place it on the counter in front of him. "Would you like anything else?"

He takes it with an arch of one thick brow. "Do you have any free time coming up soon?"

Surprised, I check the clock. "I'm taking a break in twenty minutes?"

"Perfect." He slides a five-dollar bill across the counter. "I'll be waiting by the window."

He strides off before I can give him his three dollars in change. With one eye on his broad back, I stuff the bills into the tip jar.

What could Tobias want? He came to the bakery the first day it opened, but hasn't been back since. A thrill shoots through me. Could this be a date type thing? He's never come off as the type to want to, though. He's pushy, assertive, and blunt. Not the type to take a girl out for a nice night.

At least, I don't *think* he is.

I process the next customer's order, then poke my head into the passthrough. Tally stands at the frosting counter, her brows furrowed in concentration. She wants to introduce a lavender-flavored cupcake and can't seem to get the flower pattern down.

"Hey, Tally?"

At the sound of my voice, her head jerks up, and she blinks at me for a moment, her gaze unfocused. "Yes?"

"When you're done, I need to take my break before you leave for the night."

Her eyes shift to the clock, then to the cake in her hand. "I can stay late tonight, if you wish."

Jax arrived fifteen minutes after our meeting earlier and parked himself in their usual booth. Being here, even for two hours, must be intrusive to his day.

I shake my head. "I'll be fine. You can go home as soon as I finish my break."

A soft smile spreads across her face. "I would like that. Jax is making dinner tonight for Xander, Reese, and me."

"Sounds nice."

She glances at the cupcake once more. Little blobs of purple and white frosting dot the top in a poor simulation of lavender. "Just give me a few more minutes."

"Thank you!"

As I turn back to the register, Tobias catches my attention once more. The front window frames him perfectly as he sits and calmly sips his tea. Outside, a couple of women slow down as they pass, their attention fixed to him, then veer toward the bakery's entrance.

They walk inside, giggling quietly as they sneak peeks at him. Are they going to try to flirt with my chaos demon?

My wings rustle with irritation. Tally's few minutes need to hurry up.

Trapped

Tally doesn't relieve me from the register until after the two women purchase their coffees and make their way to Tobias. So far, he's being polite but distant, and they haven't gotten up the nerve to take a seat at his table.

The second Tally walks through the swinging door, I zip into the kitchen to hang up my chef's coat, then zip right back out.

The louder of the two, a brassy redhead, now has her hand on the back of one of the empty chairs. Oh, no, she won't. I don't run toward them, but it's a somewhat embarrassing trot that brings me to Tobias. The air around the table holds the musk of desire, a scent unique to humans. Succubi and incubi learn fast what that scent means once we reach the human plane and use it to our advantage.

A human who already smells like this is much easier to beguile.

The brunette in tight yoga pants stands too close to him, near enough that even a non-sex demon can smell her lust.

Sidling around her, my hand curls over Tobias's shoulder, and I lean down to press a kiss to his cheek. "Sorry I kept you waiting."

A five o'clock shadow abrades my lips, and I take a moment to rub my cheek against it, enjoying the scratch against my skin.

His palm covers the back of my hand and presses it against his shoulder. "I enjoy watching you work, darling."

Darling? I straighten, and the happiness that started to fizzle up at the endearment fizzles back down when I find the humans still standing next to us. Guess that display didn't drive the point home to them.

Hand dropping back to my side, I force a professional smile. "Do you need help finding a table?"

The brassy one tosses her curly mane. A huntress unwilling to give up an obviously good mate without a fight. "We were just about to join your friend, here."

The blond's head jerks, too, with slightly less effect, as she adds, "But there's not enough seats. Maybe you could fetch us another?"

It's a showcase table, framed perfectly within the front window, and only designed to seat two.

I glance down at the narrow gap left between Tobias's abs and the table. I can probably wedge myself onto his lap, but it won't look very professional for my customers to see me do it.

When my focus shifts to his face, his lips twitch as he holds back a smile, and I frown at him. Why isn't he just rejecting these humans outright? Is this some kind of game? Is he waiting to see if I'll claim him?

My fingers itch to grab hold of him, but I don't like to be toyed with like this.

I click my teeth at him, and his lips purse for a moment in consideration before he stands. "Why don't the two of you take this table? We're leaving anyway."

With his tea in one hand, he cups my elbow with the other and edges us past them toward the door.

His low voice fills my ear. "You're no fun."

I glare up at him. "I don't like you testing me."

"How am I supposed to gauge your interest level

without a little prodding?" He releases me to walk through the door, then holds it open.

I fold my arms under my breasts as I stomp past him. "You could just ask."

He catches my arm, and his dark eyes bore into mine. "Adie, are you going to claim me?"

"I—" Words stick in my throat. I kind of claimed Kellen and Emil, but Tobias… Something in me balks at claiming him. Like trying to leash a wild animal that might bite me.

"And so, I'll keep testing you." His fingers lift to my face, then push the hair away from my ear as he leans down. Ozone and gentle warmth enfold me as he whispers, "You don't like others desiring me, but you won't claim me yourself. You put us in limbo, but never forget I'm designed to tip the scales. I'm the pebble that triggers the landslide, the spark that ignites the forest fire. You can't teeter on the edge forever. Something will give."

A shiver skates down my spine. The narrow ledge I balance on wobbles, and I sway toward him.

His fingers brush under my chin, dragging me that much closer to the edge. "You'll fall, it's inevitable. I just hope you're ready for the consequences when it happens."

He steps back, taking the delicious warmth of his touch with him, and I snap back to reality.

Pedestrians fill the busy street; cars line the curb. Some give us curious looks as they pass. What must I look like? Heat fills my cheeks, and quiet pants of air part my lips part. Desire heats my core, pushing at me to claim him. Claim him now. Damn the whispers of caution.

Warning bells ring my bones. Danger. Danger that doesn't come from the tempting man in front of me. This feels like yesterday in the bakery, and last night when Slater walked me back, right before Domnall grabbed us. Grabbed me.

I whip around, searching the crowded street for any sign of the fire demon.

"Adie?" Tobias touches my arm. "What's wrong?"

"I don't..." I twist to peer back at him. "Do you feel that?"

His thick brows furrow. "Feel what?"

I turn fully around and search the street behind him. Licking my lips, I taste the air, but humanity floods too close. A million emotions coat my tongue and make it impossible to pick out a single point of ill-intent directed at us.

Goosebumps pebble my arms, and I rub them. "I don't know, but I don't think we should stay here."

Tobias's gaze hardens as he, too, searches the street. "Should we go back into the bakery?"

I take a step away from the building, and the uneasy feeling sticks to me like glue. It's not focused on my shop, but on me specifically. Is Domnall out there again? Wanting to dump more power into me?

"No, I think we should go somewhere else." Somewhere away from my imps and Tally. Away from Torch and Vova.

"I'll drive." Tobias pulls a fob from his pocket, and a sleek, black luxury car beeps at the curb. Somehow, despite the busy time of night, he managed to score a spot at the curb directly in front of the bakery.

I hurry to the passenger side, my skin crawling with unease until I slide into the firm, leather seat. The edges curve up to cup my thighs, the back-rest molding to my sides, and give me a sense of security.

Tobias settles into the driver's seat, and the engine comes to life with a deep growl that vibrates my bones. Without looking, he pulls out onto the street. Heart in my throat, I grab the door handle, but the other cars part around him like water.

What the hell?

He glances at me. "Where should we go?"

"I don't know." I nibble on my lip, uncertain of what to do next. The feeling of danger sticks with us, even when Tobias shifts into a higher speed, weaving in and out of traffic. I told Tally I'd be back in an hour. "Can we just drive for a bit?"

"Sure." Tobias's hand leaves the gear shift for a second to squeeze my leg in reassurance. "Just let me know when I can stop."

He weaves in and out of traffic, the cars around him shifting lanes at exactly the right time for him to move into their spot, then filling the gap he left behind. Business buildings turn into apartments, which give way to houses with small yards.

Steadily, the sense of danger eases until, at the edge of town, it disappears completely.

I shift in my seat to peer out the rear window. "I think we out ran whatever it was."

He glances at me, his gaze calculating. "Is this the first time this has happened?"

"No." I settle back in place and stare out the windshield. "Something was off in the bakery yesterday, too. But it went away." I bite my lip in consideration before admitting. "I was called to the library, and when I came back, I was distracted."

He takes a turn through a red light and follows

the edge of the city to circle back toward Boo's Boutique Bakery. "Called to the library?"

"More like kidnapped," I mutter.

He down shifts, and the growl of the engine becomes a thrumming purr. "What did the hag want?"

"A book." I drum my fingers against my knees. "One of my cousins has it, apparently. And for some reason, that makes it my responsibility. She's calling it my *Quest*."

Interest fills his voice. "What's the prize?"

"A different book." Heat fills my cheeks. I don't want to admit to Tobias that the offer of a succubi primer to power development lured me. I'm already weak enough in his eyes.

Now, a frown mars his lips. "When did this happen?"

"Yesterday." I pull out my cell phone to check the time. "Almost twenty-four hours ago."

His head turns toward me, and his nostrils flare. "Is that why you smell funny?"

Self-conscious, I lift my arm and give it a sniff, but I still can't tell a difference from my normal scent. "Maybe?"

He stays silent for a long time as we head back into the city. Houses turn to business buildings, the setting sun casting orange and red fire across their windows. I tear my eyes from the illusion of a burning city.

At last, Tobias breaks the silence. "So, you just have to find this book and return it?"

"Yeah, I guess." I shift to find a more comfortable position on the firm seat. What originally felt like a safe hug of security now feels more like a trap. "I already checked Julian's work place, and I've never seen a book at his apartment."

"So, who's next on your list?"

Surprised, I turn to stare at him. "You want to help?"

"We can make a fast stop if you want." His hand on the steering wheel tightens. "You shouldn't keep the hag waiting."

"You have experience with her?"

He gives a short nod. "So, where are we going?"

Disappointed he doesn't want to talk about the Librarian anymore, I peer out the window to check the street sign. "Take the next left, then right on Maple. We're going to my old apartment."

∼

When I knock on my old door, it opens instantly, my cousin Sophia blocking the entrance. Clad in a skimpy green dress that matches the tips of her hair, she cocks a hip as she stares back at me. "Baby Adie, what do you want?"

I scowl. Just because I'm the youngest of our kind right now doesn't mean they need to keep calling me the baby. "Hey, Soph, I'm looking for a book. Do you mind if I come in?"

"Need to borrow a couple eroticas to get your game face on?" She steps to the side and motions for me to enter. "It's about time you stopped playing at being human."

"No, not that kind of book." I freeze as I step into the apartment.

What once was a cozy, neat space now looks like a whirlwind from the slut section of a department store crash-landed in the living room. Lace and silk undergarments litter the floor and hang from the sides of two new couches. Tiny dresses, suspended from hangers, balance on the edge of the short wall that separates the small kitchen from the dining room. Dildos and padded handcuffs poke out of baskets crammed onto a square cubby shelf.

"Oh, you brought your roommate with you?"

Sophia purrs, and I spin around to find Tobias hovering in the doorway.

I told him he could wait in the car, but it looks like curiosity got the better of him. Now, Sophia reaches out a hand to stroke over his bicep.

Intercepting her before her neon green nails make contact, I hiss, "Mine."

"No need to be greedy." She breaks my hold easily, her too bright green eyes skimming over me. "You have three of them. More than enough to share."

My wings rustle against my spine, pushing to free themselves and face this challenge.

"I'm not looking for another succubus, but thank you," Tobias rumbles from behind me.

"Too bad." Sophia holds my gaze. "I have moves baby Adie hasn't even dreamed of."

The heat of his body sinks through my clothes. "It's more fun to train someone."

His scent curls around me, enticing, and I shiver before stepping away. "No one's being trained here."

Heavy silence fills the room, and I refuse to glance back to see their expressions. The few times I let Tobias touch me, really touch me, hinted at a dominance that makes my core heat with anticipation. But giving him control makes me weak, so I keep distance between us.

I step over a pink thong and venture toward the bookcase. "Are the others home?"

"No, they're already out hunting." Sophia's high-heels clip as she follows me. "Lily has a line on a rich playboy. A couple more nights, and she should have him hooked."

"You'll need another roommate, then." I skim over the apartment, but don't immediately spot what I'm looking for.

"If you're searching for a book, we keep them all on the shelf." She nods to the cube shelf, and I sigh in resignation. I was really hoping to avoid that one.

Crouching, I pull out one of the baskets and sift through the contents. It gives off the scent of rubber and toy cleaner, and powder coats my hand by the time I reach the bottom. No book. It would really help if I knew how big the stupid thing was.

I shove the basket back in and reach for the next one. "You know, you're not supposed to store these like this."

"Yeah, whatever." She shakes back her mane of white hair, the green tips swishing over her pert ass. "I'm going to finish getting ready."

As she disappears into the single bedroom,

Tobias joins me, pulling out a basket of his own. He lifts out a book with the picture of a bound and blindfolded woman on the cover. "What does the book look like?"

"No idea." Wiping my hands on my pant legs, I pull my phone out. I was afraid I'd lose the paper the hag printed the title on, so I took a picture of it.

Holding out the phone, I show him the image, and his brow furrows. "This's what you're searching for?"

"Yeah." I perk up with excitement. "Have you heard of it?"

"Yes." The word comes out clipped. He shoves the book and basket back into place and stands. "It won't be here."

I leap to my feet. "You know who has it?"

"I can guess." He turns back to the door. "Let's get out of this place."

I hurry after him, until Sophia's voice calls me back. She leans out the bedroom doorway. "Hey, are you going to need help at your camp retreat this year?"

My lips part in surprise before I whip my phone back out and check the calendar. "Shit, I didn't realize it was already that time of year."

Tobias stops in his tracks. "What camp retreat?"

Heat fills my cheeks. "It's nothing."

"At the end of summer, baby Adie gets summoned to a camp retreat for a gaming company." She gives me an evil smirk. "They somehow got ahold of her sigil and now use it every year to ping her. She's like their good luck charm."

"It's only for one night, I can take care of it." I shove Tobias back into motion. "Let's get out of here."

"Let me know if you need a hand! I have a couple new cosplay outfits we can wear!" she calls after us as I shove Tobias out the door.

"Tell me more about the camp," Tobias demands as we head to the elevator.

"It's nothing, really." I shift from foot to foot, willing the lift to arrive faster. "I just go and whammy them into an orgy. I make up the cost in energy with the emotions they release. The whole thing is a wash."

"Do you participate?"

The elevator digs, the doors sliding open, and I leap inside. "So, who has my book? Or who do you think has it?"

"Adie." Warning fills his voice, and the metal box shakes with the first tremor of an earthquake.

I grab the handrail, suddenly unsure getting

inside the metal trap was a good idea. Tobias stalks inside and presses the button for the ground floor. The doors swish shut, and I retreat to one corner, bracing myself in case the box falls.

Death by elevator would really suck.

He crosses the short distance between us, his body making the trap even smaller. "Tell me more about this orgy."

"I don't usually participate." I lick my lips and taste ozone. "Unless I'm too low on energy. I can't whammy without energy."

"But you can't enter Dreamland." His pupils bleed outward to turn his eyes black. "You go in person."

I pant, filling my lungs with the hot air that suddenly fills the small space. My skin tingles with the brush of his power, and I know that if he touches me, I'll melt. Tobias and I have been circling each other the longest, and from that first encounter in the coffee shop, my body's craved his. My desire perfumes the air with sweet vanilla, and his nostrils flare as he takes in my scent.

He reaches out, his hot hands cupping my shoulders, and the fire of lava sinks into me.

Instantly, I choke on ash, my vision blackening around the edges. Desire flees, chased out by the all-consuming need to survive. I shove him away, sending power into my arms that slams him against the opposite wall. The elevator shakes, the wires overhead creaking with strain.

Bewildered, Tobias slowly straightens. "Adie?"

I gasp in harsh breaths, my lungs struggling for oxygen. My gut tightens and nausea rolls over me. Frantic, I claw at my throat, trying to scrape away the thick tar. Escape, I need to escape.

My wings burst from my back, catching inside my t-shirt.

"Adie, what's happening?" Tobias takes a step closer, his hands out.

I flinch away, eyes wild as I wedge myself into the corner. "Don't touch me!"

Tobias freezes in place, fear and concern on his face. I know it's Tobias, that Tobias won't hurt me, but all I see is Domnall.

The elevator doors ding open, and I hyper-speed out of there, leaving Tobias behind.

Damaged

Five blocks away, I skid to a stop next to a toy store. My arms wrap around my stomach as I gasp for air. Tobias's shocked expression sticks in my memory. How do I explain to him why I ran away?

Why *did* I run away?

Tobias's heat never bothered me in the past. Rather, it makes me excited most of the time. Even when I've feared his strength, I've never run away from it.

I blink, and Domnall's golden gaze fills my vision, hard and unyielding right before he dumped his power into me. I need to do something about that demon. Vengeance is the best cure for the kind of wound he left behind. Once I prove to myself I can stand up to him, everything else will fade away, and Tobias will be able to touch me again without me panicking.

"Excuse me, miss? Are you okay?"

Confused, I turn my head to stare at the elderly man who paused next to me. "What?"

"Are you okay?" His rheumy blue eyes crease with concern. "Do you need me to call someone for you?"

Now, even humans think I'm weak. My arms drop to my sides as I straighten. "No, everything's fine. Thank you."

"If you say so." He shuffles uncertainly for a moment, clearly not believing me.

I point to the toy store. "If you'll excuse me?"

"Sure, sure." He pats his pockets for a moment and pulls out a hard, strawberry candy. "Here, sometimes I get a little dizzy when my sugar levels drop. This might help."

"Thank you." I take it from him, the wrapper crinkling as I close it in my fist. "Have a good evening."

"You, too." With a last frown, he turns and shuffles away.

After a moment, I unwrap the candy and pop it into my mouth. Its syrupy sweetness drives away the memory of ash and actually does make me feel better.

How bad can things be when strawberry candies still exist?

Pushing away from the wall, a shiny object from inside the store catches my eye, and I smile. I lied when I told the old man I needed to go inside, but I can't resist now that I see the three-foot tall knight. Tac will love it, and maybe it will get him to stop growling at me.

Five minutes later, I stride back out of the store with the toy tucked under my arm. It cost more than I wanted to spend, but I can't wait to see the expression on Tac's face. I also picked up a bag of cheap pinwheels for the imps to steal. They'll look cute sprinkled around the bakery, but won't make a difference as they slowly go missing. Maybe I'll even branch out of my flower motif for a day and do a couple firework cupcakes to celebrate the ending of summer.

My phone beeps in my pocket with a new message, and I pull it out, expecting to see something from Tobias. Instead, Tally's name flashes on the screen.

Tally: Are you alright?

Tally: You were supposed to be back from your break fifteen minutes ago.

Guilty, I send back a fast reply.

Adie: I'm heading back now.

Tally: Smiley face.

I laugh at the spelled-out words. Has she not gotten the hang of using emojis yet?

I pick up my pace. In my panic, I ran toward the bakery instead of away. Returning now worries me. If Domnall's following me, he may have returned to the bakery after Tobias and I lost him in the car. He already dumped his energy on me. He can't be looking to dump more so fast, can he?

I push the fear aside as my wings razorblade against my spine. Let him try again. I'm prepared this time.

My shoulders stiffen with every step I take that brings me closer to Boo's Boutique Bakery, but the sense of danger never comes. I bypass the front door and walk down the narrow alley to the back parking lot to stuff the toy knight into my trunk. No reason to tempt the imps with such a shiny prize.

With the bag of pinwheels in hand, I head back to the side door and freeze.

Black paint streaks across my door in some kind of stylistic writing that's impossible to read. My vision turns red with anger. How dare some hoodlum tag *my* territory. The ugly black stripes cover my deliciously curved sigil, the paint still running. The vandals were here recently.

I storm back to the main sidewalk and search in both directions for the culprits. If I catch them tagging another business, I'll...

With a deep breath, I force my hands to unclench. If I catch them doing it again, I'll turn them into the human police. As I frequently remind Julian, we can't go around killing humans.

Which reminds me. I need to hide from my cousin that Tally's men are witches. He has a long hatred for their kind, even if these particular witches are too young to have ever participated in the Great Hunt that destroyed many of our kind and sent many more fleeing back to the demon realm in terror.

I march back to the door and quietly open it, sneaking to the pantry to find rags and cleaner. I stash the pinwheel bag under the desk before I go back outside and clean off as much of the paint as I can.

The streaks over my sigil come off with ease. The magic in the mark makes it difficult to destroy, but the paint on the actual door is a different matter.

It sticks to the metal with a tenacity that demands paint thinner.

When I step back, the already dark paint on the door makes it difficult to see the new marks. It will do until I can get to a hardware store. Graffiti can't be allowed to linger. Once one business gets tagged, it will spread like the plague. Better to nip this in the bud as quickly as possible.

Walking back inside, I throw the rags in the trashcan and return the cleaner to its shelf before I wash my hands and pull on my chef's coat. I pull a new elastic band from the desk and wind my hair into a tight bun at the back of my neck.

With one more deep breath to calm myself, I stride to the kitchen. Happy imp faces greet me, and Iris and Kelly swoop in for hugs before I make it past them.

"Master, welcome back."

"Yes, yes." I pat their arms, too tired to fight my new title. "I'm glad to be back. How were things while I was gone?"

"Tally is unhappy." Kelly's hairnet covered beard tickles as he rubs his cheek against mine. "She has failed the lavender design."

Thin arms circle my waist, and I glance down to find Jesse snuggled against my stomach. It blinks large, brown eyes up at me and chirps in greeting.

Gingerly, I pat its head, which seems to make it happier.

"Now that I'm back, why don't you all take your dinner break while I cover the front." I extricate myself with some difficulty and point to the mini-fridge under the kitchen island. "Sandwiches are already made."

Iris's rainbow head bows. "Master is kind."

I walk backward toward the swinging door. "And make sure Vova gets a fresh cupcake and milk."

"Of course." Iris bobs again.

"And please check Torch's pellet bowls." I point at Jesse. "But no expensive wood pellets. Those are for special occasions."

It blushes a dark gray, confirming my suspicions on how the fancy pellet bag got low so fast. I can't afford to feed Torch such expensive wood all the time.

Pushing through the door, I turn to find Tally at the espresso station, and Martha behind the cash register. The positions surprise me, since Martha loves the espresso machine. Does Tally think she needs more practice?

Martha spots me and smiles widely, but when she makes a move to come hug me, I give her a stern frown. Hugging in the kitchen is okay, but out here, we have to stay professional. Coworkers don't usually go around hugging each other. We don't want to look suspicious to the customers.

I walk past her to the espresso machine, where Tally stares with concentration at the thin stream of steamed milk she pours into the mug. It's an order for here, and as I watch, Tally slowly creates a leaf pattern in the foam.

I wait until she sets the milk aside before whispering, "Oh, that's beautiful."

Startled, she jumps and glances up at me, then smiles. "I saw this on TV."

My eyebrows lift in surprise. "You didn't eat someone's dreams to learn how to do it?"

"Jax says there is more of a sense of accomplishment if I learn it on my own." She turns to gaze down at the cup. "I see the merit."

"It feels good to master something on your own," I agree.

She lifts the cup and carefully carries it to the pickup counter, calling out a customer's name. When she comes back, she squeezes my arm. "I am glad you are okay. When Tobias returned without you, I worried."

"What?" I whip around to search the front of the shop, but don't find the chaos demon.

Tally shakes her head. "He could not stay, but I assured him you were well after you texted back." She studies me for a moment. "Did your date not go as planned?"

"You can say that." I hold up a hand. Jax sits in his small, corner booth, his laptop already packed and ready to go. "I'll tell you about it later. Right now, it's time for you to go home."

Tally follows my line of sight, and her face softens.

Envy shoots through me. Someday, I want that for myself. Someone to look at me with that level of love. Because that's what I'm seeing right now. Tally loves Jax in the messy, complicated way only humans can.

I nudge her shoulder. "Get going."

She only hesitates a moment before she unties her apron and runs into the kitchen to drop it in the laundry basket. I waffle on letting Martha take over her spot at the espresso machine, but decide against it. I don't know that I can act happy for the customers right now. At least behind the machine, I can hide a little.

It continues to surprise me how many people come in late at night wanting caffeine. When I first planned to serve espresso, I figured the lunch to dinner crowd would buy it, but then sales would die off. Instead, I find myself chasing customers out at closing as they linger over their cups.

Now, I switch to serving all coffee in to-go cups starting at one in the morning.

Tally comes back out of the kitchen, waves, and hurries to Jax, who slides out of the booth as he sees her coming. Hand-in-hand, they leave the store, taking with them some of the warmth in the air.

Martha soon distracts me with another espresso order and the rest of the night flies by. I rotate out with Iris and Kelly, then move back to the kitchen to go over stock and place orders for refills. Jesse and Perry scrub down the counters while I work, making the kitchen sparkle. If a health inspector ever came here, they wouldn't find a single crumb after the imps finished cleaning. I've even caught them cleaning the walls in the hallway. No surface goes untouched.

When a knock sounds at the side door, I open it to let Philip in and give him two boxes of leftover cupcakes. When Tally works late, she takes them with her and delivers them to shelters. When I work late, they go home with the imps. Once I get them settled at their new house, will they want to take the cakes with them? They sneak enough of them during the day that surely they're sick of them by the time they head home.

After they leave, I fetch the bag of pinwheels from under the desk and hide them around the store. With the lights dimmed, shadows cover the front of the shop, the streetlights bleeding through the large window, even with the blinds pulled.

A heavy silence fills the night, that odd time when most of the world sleeps.

Tonight, it makes me uneasy, and I hurry to finish the rest of my closing tasks and get out of there.

After double-checking the lock on the front door, I fetch my hoodie from the pantry, but hesitate to put it on. While the nights are getting colder, I dislike the idea of adding an additional layer of material to trap my wings. My thin t-shirt already offers enough of a hindrance.

I tie my hoodie around my waist instead, leaving my arms unencumbered, then head out the side door. Deep shadows cover the alley. I've never been worried about the lack of lights before, but tonight it makes the space between my shoulder blades itch, as if unseen eyes watch me. But when I peer back to the main street, I find it empty of even cars.

At almost three in the morning, it's the time between when the bars and clubs close and the early morning workers get up to start their day.

Steps fast, I walk to the back parking lot, digging my keys out of my pocket as I go. My old sedan sits alone within the glow of a spotlight the business next door mounted on their exterior wall. As I unlock the driver's door, I peek into the back to make sure no one broke in and now lays in wait. After the haunted house, I wouldn't be shocked to be tapped by that kind of horror movie cliche.

Sometimes, my life seems destined for bad luck.

No murderers hide in the back, and I slide behind the wheel, relieved when the engine starts on the first try. Good sense says to wait for the engine to warm, but I throw it into reverse right away and speed out of the parking lot, eager to reach the safety of my house.

With the empty streets, I hit all green lights and make it home in record time, parking my car as close to the porch as possible without being on the lawn. The tall mansion brings with it a sense of relief, and the tension eases from my shoulders. With three demons of destruction under one roof, Domnall wouldn't dare to come there.

I climb out of my car, go to the trunk, and pull out Tac's new toy. I can't wait to see his adorable face when he sees it. Maybe I'll finally get some relief from my dreams plagued with knights.

Tucking it under one arm, I walk to the porch, the house key out and ready.

With my foot on the first step, I freeze as the scent of ozone reaches me, followed by the burn of fire.

A quiet voice rumbles out of the shadows. "I've been waiting for you."

F*CK TARTS

"I've been waiting for you."

At the quiet words, I hold back a shriek and fumble the toy under my arm. Whipping around, I find Tobias sitting on a chair in the corner of the porch. Relief rushes over me, thankful it's not Domnall setting a trap where I feel safest. Anger quickly follows.

Did he drag one of the chairs up from the basement for the sole purpose of skulking? Why not just wait inside?

Still a little shaky, I glare at him. "Are you trying to give me a heart attack?"

"You worried me earlier." He stands and stalks closer. "I don't like to be worried."

"So, what? Your revenge is to scare the crap out of me?"

His head tilts, shadows over his face. "Why are you scared?"

I toss my head. "Um, because you're hiding like some gargoyle on the porch?"

"I've been out here for a while. Long enough for my scent to fill the space. You should have known I was here right away." His head tilts the other direction as he studies me. "So, what has you so afraid?"

I rise onto my toes, shoulders back. "I'm not afraid."

As a catalyst demon, Tobias smells a bit like all the demons of destruction, depending on his mood. No wonder that, for one heart-stopping moment, I mistook him for Domnall. His anger leaks like the slow spread of a forest fire across the porch.

But the hint of fire makes my bones shiver with phantom pain.

Instinctively, I edge away from it as the memory of burning alive rears back to the surface. The blisters on my skin, the crackle of my bones. A shudder rolls through me. Not again. Never again.

The fire pulls away from me, and cool night air sweeps in. My eyes snap open in surprise, and I don't know at what point I closed them. The hard press of the banister digs into my ass, and I realize I backed all the way across the porch from Tobias, an unconscious retreat that shouts louder than my earlier protest.

Tobias stands at the opposite side of the porch, his powers banked as low as he can manage in his current state. I haven't skimmed from him recently, and his energy levels build steadily with every day that passes.

We stare at each other in silence. I can't bring myself to be near him. If I can't do my job as his succubus, will he turn to another?

My wings rustle in protest. *No*, Tobias is *mine*.

I take a step toward him, then another. My limbs shake with the effort to force myself forward, but when I reach the place where his fire scent lingers, I can't make myself take another step. I shake with the strain of staying in place, to not retreat back to my corner, to not hide from Tobias.

A short gasp of effort escapes, and fire fills my lungs. With a whimper, I break and retreat back to my side of the porch. I can't do it. I hate myself for the weakness, and I hate Domnall more for doing this to me.

I hug Tac's toy knight to my chest, taking comfort in its rigid pieces.

Pain fills Tobias's voice. "What did I do to make you afraid?"

My chest aches and I lick my lips, surprised when I find soft, supple skin instead of blisters. Unwilling to let him think he hurt me, I whisper, "It's not you."

He moves closer, and I rear back in panic. He freezes, and the scent of fire increases with his anger. "It's not me? How can you say that when you can't stand to be near me?"

"Can you–" With a gasp, I turn my head away to find clean air. "The scent–" My gut clenches with nausea, and I grab the banister, willing down the bile.

"Stay here. Do *not* run away again," Tobias commands, and the front door opens and closes.

After he steps into the house, the air on the porch begins to clear, filling with the fresh smell of dew on the grass, the chill of fall, soon to arrive. Shivering, I set the toy knight on the floor and unwrap my hoodie, tugging it on. I want to go inside, to burrow into my pillow nest and sleep until my alarm clock wakes me again.

Instead, I stay put, my arms wrapped around my stomach and my head down.

The front door opens once more, and two sets of

footsteps echo against the wooden planks, one hard heeled and the other with the quiet shush of bare feet.

I peek up, and Emil blinks at me tiredly, his white hair rumpled from sleep. He wears only sweatpants, his milky chest bare and shimmering with the hint of frost. In contrast, Tobias stands at his shoulder, still fully clothed in the suit he wore on our date this evening. He hadn't even changed when he came home. Was he waiting out here the entire night?

"What's going on?" Emil mumbles as he glances between us.

Tobias's brows pinch together with unhappiness. "Adie's afraid of me."

Emil straightens into alertness, and the creak of icebergs fills the air. "What did you do?"

"Nothing!" I rush to intercept the potential fight. "I'm not afraid of Tobias. This is a misunderstanding."

"Liar." Tobias moves around Emil, coming closer, and I scuttle away before I can stop myself. He stops and gestures at me. "See?"

With a contemplative look, Emil walks to me, bringing with him the clean scent of ozone and ice. When I don't run, he slowly wraps his arms around me. Shuddering, I bury my nose against his neck and fill my lungs with frost.

Cold air ruffles my hair as he sniffs me in return before he pulls back. "You still smell off."

He bends and inhales close to my lips. Surprised, I turn away, but he catches my chin, lifting my face.

Hard eyes stare down at me. "Open your mouth."

I press my lips into a mutinous line. No, he will *not* smell my breath after a day of work.

He leans closer, his nose brushing against mine. It brings his mouth within kissing distance, and my heart rate picks up. His thumbs stroke my jaw, then my throat, before coming back up to cup my cheek. Despite knowing what he's up to, the silent tease of the almost kiss lures me in, and when his breath fans across my lips, they part, eager to have him in my mouth.

After a long day of work, his icy tongue sounds refreshing.

But instead of the sweet caress of lips and teeth, his thumb slides into my mouth. Almost as good. I suck on it, tongue flicking over the rough pad and the hard curve of nail. For a moment, snow flurries across his pupils, then he presses down, his thumb hooked behind my teeth to drag my mouth open.

"This is not sexy at all," I mumble around his appendage.

When he dips down, nostrils flared, I bite him, but he ignores the nip of pain to inhale deeply.

"You're being gross." The words come out garbled, and I jerk my head away to scrub a hand over my mouth. "What are you doing?"

Emil steps back, his arms folded over his chest and his expression inscrutable. "I think it's time you told us about what happened last night. Why you smelled like fire and baby powder and another demon."

A few steps away, Tobias stiffens. "What other demon?"

I glare at Emil. "I told you it was nothing."

"You're lying." He leans close, his words fogging in the space between us. "Didn't you say people in relationships don't lie to each other?"

"I'm dealing with it," I growl through clenched teeth.

Tobias stomps closer but stops outside of touching range. "If this has anything to do with why you're afraid of me all of the sudden, we have a right to know."

My hands open and close into helpless fists. What can I tell them that doesn't break my word to protect Slater?

"Last night, outside the bakery"—I pick out the words carefully, my eyes darting between them—"a demon named Domnall grabbed me."

They exchange angry glances as they recognize the name. The scent of forest fires and avalanches flood the patio, and I take shallow breaths to fight down the instinctive need to run. Danger shivers in my bones, but their anger isn't for me. At least, I don't think it is.

Emil motions for me to continue.

Licking my lips, I taste embers on the wind, and my stomach rolls. My arms cross over my stomach as I hug myself. "I think he's a destruction demon like you guys?"

"Not quite," Tobias bites off. He takes a step away, now conscious of what his scent does to my fight-or-flight instincts.

"Well, he needed to dump his power or something, so he grabbed me and—"

"I'll destroy him." Tobias spins to the stairs, and I dart in front of him, my own anger adding spice to the air.

I throw my arms up to block the opening in the porch. "No! This revenge is *mine*."

He halts in his tracks to stare at me. Black without a hint of white floods his eyes. "You can't handle him. Obviously."

Rage turns my vision red at the edges, and I rise onto my toes, my chest puffing out. "You won't take this from me."

"He touched what is *ours*." Fine tremors shake the porch with his anger. "We cannot let this go."

Caution fills Emil's voice. "Tobias—"

"Adie is clearly marked under our contract," he snaps, glaring over his shoulder at the ice demon. "He should not have touched our property."

The red takes over, and the energy ball in my core explodes outward to flood my limbs. My claws rip through Tobias's shirt as I slam him backward into the side of the house. My feet leave the ground, my clogs falling away, before I sink talons into the hard siding on either side of his body.

Leaning into his angry face, I hiss, "This is not about you, Tobias. This was not done *to you*. We are not *property* and *owner*, we are equal under *contract*."

"Easy, Adie, easy." Cold hands hesitantly touch my arms.

I twist to bare my teeth at Emil. He won't stop me from putting this catalyst demon in his place.

Headlights splash over the porch as Kellen pulls into the driveway and swings toward the garage at the rear of the house. He must spot us because he chirps to a stop, and his engine cuts off, the lights vanishing.

In my disorientation, Tobias shoves me off, and only Emil's hold on my arms stops me from hitting the ground. Gingerly, Emil sets me back on my feet, and my bare toes curl against the rough planks of wood. Kellen's sudden appearance wiped out my rage, and now I sidle to put Emil between me and Tobias, worried at what the catalyst demon will do after my attack.

In retrospect, that was not the smartest path of action.

Kellen shoves his door open, and the dome light flares to life. He climbs out and slams the door shut, his steps heavy as he stomps up the steps to join us on the porch.

Concern and exhaustion fill his voice. "What's going on?"

At once, Tobias's and Emil's anger emerges again, directed at the storm demon now.

Ice spreads from beneath Emil's feet as he accuses, "You brought Adie to Domnall's attention."

"Hey, now." Kellen lifts his hands, palms out. "That was an accident, and she left right away. I doubt he even remembers her."

"Oh, he remembers her." Tobias straightens, tugging at the tattered remains of his button-up shirt. "He attacked her."

Lightning crackles across Kellen's pupils. "When?"

"Last night." Emil turns to me. "Outside the bakery."

"*When?*" Kellen repeats as his focus shifts to me.

The ground rocks beneath my feet and I can't tell if it's Tobias's anger manifesting as an earthquake or the fear my next words will sentence a friend to death. "After I got back to the bakery."

Kellen's eyelids drop to shutter his gaze, and he slowly spins his car keys around his finger. "How long after you got back? Did you go inside and come back out for something? What time, *precisely*, did this happen?"

"I'm not sure about the time." I shrug my shoulders uneasily. "The Librarian was pestering me, and I stopped to yell at a signboard."

If I hoped to distract him with that moment of stupidity in my life, I fail.

He catches his keys in his fist. "Where was Slater when this happened?"

Here's where being a demon sucks. If they can tell when I lie, then I can't lie. But if I tell the truth, Slater's dead. Which means I need to be creative with my truths.

I force myself to meet Kellen's eyes. "Slater left before Domnall dumped all his power into me."

Truth. Slater ran for help before Domnall unloaded everything. One little word to turn a lie into reality.

Some of the tension eases from Kellen's shoulders. "How did you escape?"

"He caught me off guard." Truth. "But once he started dumping, he was distracted, and I escaped and ran to hide in the bakery." Another truth. No reason to bring up that Xander did the distracting. "Once there, I put the bakery on lockdown, and Domnall didn't try to follow."

At least, not as far as I was aware after I passed out. Tally said the barrier went down after I lost consciousness. If he wanted to continue the power dump, he wouldn't have had to try hard. Which tells me he offloaded enough to move along.

Kellen's mouth opens, undoubtedly to try to better pin down my answers, but Tobias interrupts. "Earlier today, you thought someone was following you. Was that Domnall?"

"I don't know." I shiver at the memory. "I've never felt another demon nearby. I usually have to sniff them out."

Thoughtful, Emil's focus zeros in on my middle. "Perhaps because some of his power still lingers in you?"

"Maybe?" I pat my stomach, but can't detect the residue they keep picking up on. "Though, I puked most of it out. That stuff was nasty."

"You threw it up?" Alarm fills Kellen's voice. "What did you do with it after that?"

My brows furrow together. Yeah, expelling energy isn't the norm for succubi and incubi, but it happens sometimes. Especially when there are clashing energies involved. "I washed it down the sink. Why?"

"I'm sure it's fine." Tobias slices a hand through the air. "But why would Domnall follow Adie around? What could he want with her?"

"He's hunting." Kellen's curt words seem to mean something different to Tobias and Emil than they do to me.

I point at Kellen. "He better stay away from my cousins." Guilt rolls through me, and I dig my phone out of my pocket and pull up the group messenger. "I'm sending out a warning to everyone. He won't find another unsuspecting succubi or incubi around here."

My fingers hesitate over the keyboard. How to describe Domnall so they know to steer clear?

Kellen's fingers cover my screen, and I jump, startled he got so close without me noticing. "Adie, it's okay. If he dumped his energy, it's unlikely he'll need to do so again. Domnall's power doesn't recharge the same way ours does."

Confused, I lower my phone. "But he's a destruction demon, right?" My focus shifts to Emil. "He needs one of my kind to syphon off his energy, right? It's part of the agreement you all struck with the higher-ups."

"Domnall made his own bargain." Tobias's arms fold over his chest. "Part of that was to stay out of our territories."

Chagrined, Kellen rubs the back of his neck. "I gave him a pass." At the other's outraged expressions, his hands drop. "I *did* email you both with an update."

Emil immediately pats the empty pockets of his

sweatpants, and Tobias pulls a phone from his slacks. The two huddle together, the screen's light illuminating their faces.

With them distracted, Kellen reaches for me, his face serious. "Adie, I'm so sorry being with me brought his attention to you. I will deal with this personally."

Annoyed, I shake off his touch. "I'll deal with it myself." Leaning past him, I glare at Tobias. "You hear that, you thick-headed asshole? *I* will deal with Domnall."

"Now, Adie..." Kellen reaches for me again, petting my arms. "Domnall's too powerful for yo–"

"Oh, my god, you testosterone-laden fuck tarts!" Jerking away, I stomp across the porch to where my toy knight lays in a metal heap against the rail. I scoop it up into my arms before I spin to face them once more, the armor-covered toy in front of my chest like a shield.

I glare at each of them in turn. "If *any* of you dare to exact revenge on my behalf, I will file claims against all of you. I will wrap you up in demon court and make a complete nuisance of myself for the next year. At which point, I will leave, and you won't be able to find another succubi or incubi anywhere to fill my spot."

The toy gives a shriek of protest as my tight grip bends the armor. "Do *not* test me on this. My mentor is Landregath the Great Devourer, and he will back me on this one! You'll be *lucky* if cousin Cassandra accepts your call!"

My chest heaves as I take in their shocked expressions then stomp to the door and shove it open.

Hand still on the knob, I turn back. "And none of you are getting cuddles!"

And with that, I slam the door shut, leaving them on the porch to get over themselves.

Tac's Knight

"**A**nd then, they *dared* to tell me they'd take care of it!" I shout into the phone. "Can you believe the nerve?"

"Darling, you're making a fuss over nothing," Julian sighs. "Just let the big bads sort it out amongst themselves. No reason to risk your own feathers."

"*My* revenge!"

"Yes, yes. So you said. The claim is yours."

I stomp back and forth across my bedroom, my wings out and flared wide. "I don't feel like you're taking this seriously."

"I'm happy you're worried, but most of us aren't stupid enough to get yanked into some icky alley," he drawls. "It's survival one-oh-one, darling. We are sexy, sexy demons, and that makes others think they can take advantage of us."

"But that's what I'm *saying*, Julian!" Frustrated, I throw myself onto the couch next to my bed. "This guy's bad news. If you see him coming, go the other way."

"What did you say he looked like again?" Tone bored, Julian sounds like he only half listens to me.

"Dark hair, kind of golden eyes. Tall. Muscular."

"Sounds yummy."

"He almost killed me," I seethe. "If I hadn't escaped, I would be ash right now."

Interest perks Julian's voice. "What did you say his name was, again?"

"Domnall." I search my memory. "Domnall MacAteer."

"The name doesn't ring any bells." He hums quietly under his breath in thought. "Gold eyes you said? And ash?"

"Like he was dumping the leftovers of a freaking forest fire into me." A shudder of revulsion shoots through me at the memory.

"Interesting."

I sit up straight. "Wait, you know something, don't you?"

"Possibly," he hedges. "I need to look into a couple things first."

"Tell me."

"Be patient. It might be nothing." Excitement thrums through his voice, though. Far more than I've heard from him in recent years.

"Julian," I caution, "stay away from this guy. He's bad news, and you're not at your best right now."

"Don't worry about me, darling," he purrs into the phone. "I hit up a sorority party a couple hours ago. I'm *bursting* with energy."

Relief washes through me. I don't like to see Julian at less than his perky best. "I'm glad to hear that."

"You should come next time. So much youthful energy."

A smile spreads across my lips. "I'll pass."

"Of course you will." He releases a put-upon sigh. "You're so boring, darling."

"Will you spread the word?"

"Yes, though I'm sure your email was sufficient." He yawns into the phone. "Anything else? Or can I go back to reveling in all this delicious energy?"

"Go back to sleep. Sorry, I woke you."

"Hey, Adie?"

Julian's serious tone catches me off guard. "Yes?"

"Send me a nude pic of that storm demon of yours. I want to add it to my scrapbook album."

"Good*night*, Julian." I hang up on his laughter, glad he's in a better mood.

But he won't be getting any of the pics I snapped of Kellen walking around naked in his bedroom across from mine. I cradle my phone to my chest. Those are just for *my* personal viewing.

Throwing the phone onto the other end of the couch, I peek up over the back to stare at my open doorway. Since I stormed up to my bedroom, I haven't heard the guys come into the house.

Are they having a manly pow-wow on the porch? Trying to figure out how to punish Domnall without me figuring it out?

I wish my rage hadn't made me threaten them, but now that I spoke the words, I have to follow through. Demons take their revenge seriously. As the injured party, my claim comes before theirs.

My blood still boils at Tobias calling me their *property*. I may be a contracted succubus in this house, but I'm not a freaking piece of furniture.

Speaking of furniture...

Climbing off the couch, I circle to one side and grab the padded arm, tugging it toward the door. It's about time I stake out my place in the living room. Much as I enjoy sharing the couch with Emil, sometimes I want more than the corner.

The wooden legs screech across the floor, and the two-seater sticks in the doorway for a moment until I wedge it up onto two legs and yank it through. As I walk it down the first step, it makes a loud thumping noise that echoes through the house. I could expend energy to make this easier, but I like the racket it makes.

No more stealthy invasion ideas for me. This is a hostile takeover.

Adeline Boo Pond is here to stay.

At least for the year. Then I'll check their asshole meters again to see if I want to sign on for another year. I'll prepare their contracts in advance and make them my bitches.

The couch slams down on the second-floor landing, and a creak from the left draws my attention to Emil's bedroom. His door swings open, and Tac peeks out, his tufted ears swiveling at the noise during a time of day most of the house usually sleeps.

I drop the couch, my hands moving to my hips as I glare at him. "What? You going to give me flack, too?"

His nostrils ruffle, and one side of his lip curls up with the beginning of a growl.

Stabbing a finger at him, I yell, "Don't you give me that bullshit! I've had enough of being told I smell weird!"

Instantly, his lip uncurls, and he drops to his belly, his saucer-size green eyes wide.

"That's what I thought." With a firm nod, I lift the couch once more and drag it to the next flight of stairs.

My thighs burn from walking backward, and I make it down three more steps before Tac's ears appear over the arm opposite me.

I pause. "What are you doing?"

Slowly, one black paw creeps up and pushes down on that side of the couch to stick it in place.

"Stop that," I growl as I tug on my end.

In answer, he peeks over the top of the couch.

I glare and yank on my end, but it stays in place. "Tac, I'm warning you."

His wings rustle, and the paw slowly disappears.

With a huff, I pull the couch down a couple more steps, then stumble as it surges forward with a hard push. I drop it and grab the railing to stop myself from falling. "Tac, stop!"

His wings rustle again, then he leaps straight up,

his body brushing the ceiling, and lands in the center of the couch with a satisfied rumble. With his added weight, the couch slides down a couple more steps, then stops. Tac hops on the cushions to dislodge it, and my heart slams into my throat as it teeters on the edge of the steps.

I spin and hyper-speed down the stairs to get out of the way as the couch turns into a sled that Tac rides to the bottom, where it flips on its side and spills the stupid beast into the living room in a tangle of wings and flailing paws.

The front door slams open, and the guys rush around the entryway wall.

"Adie, are you okay?" Kellen demands as he arrives first.

I wave him off, concerned Tac hurt himself, but the beast rolls to his feet, shaking his large, wedge-shaped head as he settles his wings against his back.

"What's going on?" Tobias demands as he takes in the flower-printed couch that semi-blocks the stairway.

"I'm bringing my couch down." Now that I know Tac's safe, I shoulder him out of the way to right my sofa and move it in front of the fireplace. Back to them, I add, "This is *my* spot."

"Are you sure you want it there?" Strain fills Emil's voice.

An evil grin spreads over my face. Emil won't like the mismatched furniture.

As if to prove my point, he adds, "We can buy you a couch if you really want one for yourself. You don't need to give up your personal seating."

Twisting, I give him a hard stare. "Are you saying my furniture isn't allowed out here?"

"No, of course not." His horror-filled gaze sticks to the couch. "But I was considering remodeling again..."

"No," Kellen and Tobias snap at the same time.

Emil's focus shifts to the broken chair propped against one wall. "But Tobias needs a new chair anyway..."

Kellen slaps him on the shoulder. "Adie and I are taking care of that." He turns to me with an easy grin. "Isn't that right?"

My wings rustle with irritation. I still blame Kellen for the broken chair. He should take full responsibility, but I bite out an unenthusiastic, "Right."

Kellen rubs his palms together. "Do you need help?"

"No."

His eyebrows lift. "Are you sure?"

I turn back to the couch. "I'm fine."

"Don't be like that." A warm body drapes over my back, followed by a rush of static. "We're sorry we implied you couldn't take care of your own revenge. Aren't we, guys?"

Mutters come from Emil and Tobias that don't even come close to apologies.

"You did more than *imply*." I try to shrug Kellen off, but he clings to me, his arms draped over my shoulders to make moving difficult. "Get off."

"I'd love to." His chin burrows through my hair until he finds skin, and he peppers lightning-filled kisses along my neck. "You promised to cuddle with me tonight, right?"

"I did no such thing." Squirming, I get out from under him and spin, my arms folded under my breasts. "I won't be swayed on this. You guys were out there scheming something. What? Are you going to distract me with hot sex while they"–I fling an arm in Tobias's and Emil's direction–"go hunt down Domnall?"

Kellen's head turns toward the other two, a stupid grin on his pretty face. "You hear that? My sex *is* distracting."

"I told you she wouldn't go for it." Emil stomps

into the room and heads for the kitchen. "Anyone else need a drink?"

Tobias follows him. "I'll take some chamomile tea."

"Do we have any whiskey?" Kellen catches my hand and drags me to the archway. "A hot toddy sounds good right now."

My feet drag. "I need to go to bed."

"After you just worked up a sweat moving that couch downstairs?" Kellen swings our linked arms. "You need something to settle down."

"I'm settled enough."

"Is someone pouting?" He tugs me forward and slaps me lightly on the ass. "Come on. Have a drink with us."

I glare as Emil and Tobias settle onto the bar stools that line the kitchen island. "If your new plan is to get me drunk so I don't notice what you're all up to, it won't work."

Tobias props his elbows on the countertop. "I don't think we have enough booze in the house for that."

Most demons have a high tolerance for alcohol. My succubus nature turns everything I consume into energy, so if I want to get drunk, it's a matter of consuming faster than my body converts. Expensive and ultimately pointless when I can get a better high from glutting on passion.

No, if demons want to alter their reality, they use demon-based substances, like the succubus tear I bargained to Kellen when I first accepted the request that I move in. Expensive and hard to obtain, it's worth far outweighed the energy I stole from his club, but I hadn't had much else to offer. I have a box of feathers stashed in my room for a rainy day. They don't fall from my wings often, and I save every one of them for future bartering needs.

I glance at Kellen, curious if he ever drank my tear or if he's saving it for his own future bargains.

Kellen meets my gaze. "What would you like to drink? Anything in the kitchen is open tonight."

On his stool, Emil straightens with alarm but keeps his mouth shut. It almost makes me want to choose one of his fancy hot chocolates. He hoards them like a dragon does gold, and there's a white chocolate strawberry one I've had my eye on for a while now.

Licking my lips, I pull myself free of Kellen's grasp and circle wide around Tobias to the stool on the other side of Emil.

The scent of fire still clings to Tobias, and I can't bring myself to be near him. Which makes me angry with myself. Tobias isn't Domnall, but my instincts scream at me to run.

I slide onto the stool and grip the counter, my head down. Right now, I'm not my biggest fan. This makes me feel weak, to be swayed by my primal urges.

Kellen bustles around to the stovetop and flicks on the burner under the kettle. "What will it be, Adie?"

My voice comes out small. "Chai tea, please."

"Done." He walks to the cabinet we keep the mugs in and pulls out four, lining them up on the counter. A tea bag of chamomile goes into the first one, a generous splash of whiskey into the next. To that, he adds honey and a cinnamon stick for good measure. A blind grab pulls a packet of chocolate mint from Emil's drawer, then he fetches the generic tub of chai powder from my cupboard and scoops in four generous spoons full of powder into the last mug.

Tac joins us in the kitchen and flops down under the dining table where his chomped up Tiffany's lamp waits. With one large paw, he drags it over to rest his chin on top and closes his eyes. It reminds me of the toy I bought for him.

I hop off the stool once more. "I'll be right back."

Running up to my room, I grab the toy knight from the side of my bed and hurry back downstairs. When I walk back into the kitchen, the guys halt their hushed conversations, and I give them a displeased frown as I go to Tac. His eyes slit open at my approach, a thin line of green that widens as he spots the shiny armor. His tail thumps against the floor in excitement, and he crawls out from beneath the table.

I hold the toy out. "You want the knight?"

His left foot lifts, talons extending.

"Who's a good demon kitty?" I shake the knight back and forth, and his eyes track the movement. "Who misses the old days?"

"I sure do," Kellen mumbles.

"Shush." I turn my head to stick my tongue out at him. "This isn't about you."

Tac takes my distraction and lunges forward to grab the knight by one leg. Metal crunches, and the beast darts out of the kitchen, dragging the toy along.

Emil scowls. "I better not end up with armor shards in my bed."

My hands move to my hips. "Did you get glass shards?"

His frosty gaze drops to the mangled lamp under the table. "No."

"Then you'll be fine." The kettle whistles, steam pouring from its spout, and I scoot back to my place on the stool next to him. "Ever since I started practicing the whole desire reading thing, he's been plaguing me with dreams of knights."

Interest fills Emil's voice. "You've been practicing?"

"Well, yeah." I fold my arms on the counter and lean forward, tired and ready for bed. "You said you'd need me for bank meetings at some point, right?"

"I did." He studies me. "How's it going so far?"

I drop my head onto my arms. "Tac's the only one I'm getting more than sex from."

"You'll get there." He rubs a chilly palm over my back.

"I want to get there faster."

In the middle of adding spoons to the mugs for stirring, Kellen pauses to waggle his eyebrows at me. "I can help with that."

I turn my nose up. "It wasn't much help yesterday."

His lips purse in affront. "Did you *try?*"

"Well, no..." Domnall interrupted us in the middle of it then attacked me afterward.

With the power an uneasy mass in my stomach, I hadn't felt up to practicing mind reading. Getting through the day was difficult enough. And Tobias showed up to take me out. He hadn't smelled like fire at first. In fact, he rarely smelled like fire up until recently.

"There you have it." Kellen pushes the mugs across the counter, one in front of each of us. "We'll just have to try again."

"Maybe she needs someone with more power to offer right now," Emil murmurs as he slowly stirs his hot chocolate. "The summer storms have passed. You won't regenerate as fast now."

Lightning flickers across Kellen's pupils. "Oh, and you think the coming fall will give you an extra boost?"

Frost coats the spoon in Emil's fingers. "It does lead into my most powerful season."

Fire nips at my nose as Tobias's anger surges back to life. "I'm powerful year-round."

I cup a hand over my lower face and lean past Emil to focus on the catalyst demon. "Why do you smell like that so much?"

Surprise crosses his features. "Like what?"

"Forest fires."

He shrugs. "It's the season for forest fires. Everything's drying out right now."

"Can you tone it down?"

"Can you get it through your head I'm not Domnall?"

My wings razorblade against my spine. "It's not my head that's having the issues."

"You should have better control of your instincts."

I stand on the bottom rung of my stool to glare down at him. "Go back to smelling like volcanoes and landslides!"

His stool skitters against the tiles as he thrusts to his feet. "I can't control it!"

"Neither can I!"

Hot chocolate pinched between two fingers, Emil stands and moves out from between us.

Tobias and I square off, and he gestures at me. "You had no problem recovering after Torch almost killed you. Why are you so affected this time?"

"Because Torch *loves* me! He didn't mean to hurt me! Domnall used me like a trash can to dump his waste in!"

Tobias rears back, his eyes wide. "And now you

think I'll do the same?"

"No." My arms loop around my stomach in self-defense. "But this is different somehow."

His thick eyebrows pinch together. "Different how?"

I squeeze myself tighter. My bones hum with pent-up energy, as if I'll fly apart at any moment. "I don't *know*!"

"Adie, you know I like you, right?"

"No! I don't, actually!" I bite my lip for a moment before my voice quiets. "You yell at me a lot. And you're not gentle at all. And, yeah, you came to take me out earlier, but..." I peer down at him, then glance at Emil and Kellen. They stand side-by-side, sipping from their mugs with rapt attention. My focus shifts back to Tobias. "I can't read you, and you don't try to sweet talk me or anything. I know you want sex, but as far as I know, you'd want that from any succubus that can drain you."

The emotion slides from Tobias's face to leave him blank. "Is that really what you think of me?"

Now the air grows heavy, a mudslide on the precipice of falling, but it brings me no comfort. When I flick my tongue out to taste the mood, it holds the bitter edge of pain.

Uncertain, I check with the other two, but they refuse to meet my eyes. Doubt shoots through me. How did this turn from me being angry at them to them being mad at *me*? I'm ruining whatever balance we found in the household, all because of what Domnall did to me.

"I don't go to your cousin's homes and fix their ovens, Adie. I don't give leniency to your cousins if they break my possessions." Tobias steps closer, and I lock my knees to stay firm as he leans in. "And when I give you my power, it will be because you beg me to fill you. When you melt for me, it will be with pleasure. And if I hurt you, it will be because you ask me to."

My pulse spikes, my throat suddenly thick with some emotion I can't pinpoint. Tobias's words make my body burn, but not with the memory of ash.

He turns away and heads for the door. "I'm done for the night. Emil, we're leaving early in the morning."

He disappears, and Emil releases a heavy sigh. Taking his mug, he follows Tobias out, softly calling for Tac.

My legs shake with effort, and I slump onto the stool. To the floor, I mumble, "I don't understand what's going on."

"Figure it out." Kellen pats me on the shoulder as he passes.

For a moment, I hold my breath and wait for him to bring up cuddling again. When he doesn't, relief and despair tighten my throat.

I don't know these men well enough to recognize Tobias's gestures as his form of courting. I thought he was just being nice the few times he helped me out, but I should have realized my mistake in that assumption. Few demons are nice without reason. But even if I made the connection, how could I know it meant he liked me as more than a possible sex partner?

While I met Tobias first, I've spent the least amount of time with him since moving in.

What do I know about him besides he dislikes sweets and he's good at fixing ovens and furniture?

Nothing. And somehow that feels wrong. I've lived with them for almost two months now, but I've been so busy with starting up the bakery, then working there, that I skimped on getting to know my roommates.

That needs to end. I'm going to learn more about all of them, even if I have to pry the information out one kernel at a time.

Fallen & Can't Get Up

Tac wakes me long before my alarm does as he bounces up onto the bottom two-thirds of my bed. My pillow nest shakes, letting in a ray of sunlight to blind me. I could have sworn I closed my shutters last night.

Beneath me, the mattress vibrates as Tac lets out a contented rumble, followed by the crunch of metal. I let out a grumble of my own and reach for the dislodged pillow to fill the gap. No way I'm getting up early today. Maybe I should ask Emil to put Tac back in his room after he showers. Not that it will matter. Even without hands, the beast somehow manages to open doors all on his own.

Kitty telekinesis?

I push the pillow back down to squint out at him. What are the odds he can move things with his mind?

Tac glances up, the knight's head wedged between his back teeth, and his ears swivel toward me. Quickly, I stuff the pillow back in place, but it's too late. The bed bounces as Tac wiggles closer to my nest, and moist kitty breath puffs through the cracks in the pillows.

I curl tighter around my purple sequined square. "Go away, Tac. I'm sleeping."

He chuffs, and a massive weight presses me down into the mattress as he climbs on top of my pillow mound.

"Get off!" I yell as the beast stands on top of me.

Ignoring me, Tac stomps around, his head shoveling down through the various sized pillows to find me inside.

"Tac, down!" Emil commands.

Instantly, Tac launches off my back, and I shoot upright, pillows bouncing everywhere. Emil stands in my doorway, a towel draped loosely around his waist. Drops of frozen water pebble on his shoulders and reflect the sun into tiny rainbows that play off his milky skin.

Tac stands in the space between us, his wings flapping gently against his back as he waffles on what to do. At last, he returns to the bottom of the bed long enough to clamp onto the knight's leg with his teeth, then pads to Emil's side.

Emil strokes his head absently, his gaze fixed on me. "You okay?"

I blow hair from my face. "I wish people would stop asking that."

He stiffens into an icy statue. "Sorry to worry about you."

My mouth drops open in shock as he spins on one heel to leave, Tac close behind. Oh, no. *No, no, no, no.* I'm not alienating Emil, too.

I spring out of the bed, and my foot lands on one of the fallen pillows. My leg slides out from under me at the same time my arms pinwheel before the world turns horizontal, and I slam onto my ass with a hard thump. Pain shoots up my spine, and I fall onto my side in the fetal position.

Why, life?

Emil's footsteps pause, then he slowly walks back to the doorway. Patting the floor, I find the corner of a pillow and drag it over my head. Why does he have to witness this?

"Adie?"

My tailbone throbs and I fight not to sniffle. "Yes?"

After a long pause, he says, "I won't ask."

My nose and eyes sting, and I mumble into the pillow.

"What was that?"

When I peek at him, he stands in the center of the doorway, his toes at the threshold. I lower the pillow farther. "I'm not okay."

The corner of his mouth twitches. "Have you fallen and you can't get up?"

I throw the pillow at him, and it soars over his head. "Don't laugh at me!"

"Can I come into your room?"

My heart lurches. I haven't let any of the guys into my room. It's my sanctuary in the house. The one place that belongs to just me. But my ass and back hurt, and the idea of standing right now makes me cringe. I could just lay on the hard floor until the pain subsides, but Emil tempts me with his hidden offer of assistance. He didn't come straight out and ask if I need help because that implies I'm weak. Despite everything, he treads carefully around my feelings.

Warm tingles fill my limbs. "You can come in." As his foot lifts, I rush to add, "But, just for today."

He enters my room with a slight displacement of air, the warmth of morning giving way to his frost.

He circles around my prone form, and the mattress creaks behind me.

Confused, I lift an arm into the air, waving it for his attention. "Um, Emil?"

"Oh, did you need *help*?" He practically purrs the word, and a pillow bounces off my back, followed by the rustle of my blanket. "Oh, I see now why Tac comes here to nap after I leave for work."

"What are you—" I bolt upright, then groan in pain. Maybe it's worth the energy expense to hurry this healing along. I spindle out a thin line, and the ache eases away.

On my knees, I turn to find Emil burrowed into my bed, his head on my purple sequined pillow. He watches me through half-lidded eyes. "This is quite cozy."

"Who said you could lay there?" I push to my feet, my hand rubbing my lower back. "I let you come in so you could—"

"*Help* you?" He plumps the pillow behind his head. "I thought you were a strong succubus who didn't need help from others."

Somehow, this reeks of a trap. He's using my current misfortune to bring back our discussion from last night.

My hands move to my hips. "Shouldn't you be at work?"

"Tobias is handling it." He pats the space next to him in invitation. "It's still early for you. Come back to bed."

"I don't want to." Annoyed, I bend to pick up the pillows from the floor.

It will take forever to get my nest put back in order. Each pillow has its place in the structure. If even one is out of alignment, the whole nest fails.

Stomping to the bed, I throw my armful near the headboard.

Cool fingers wrap around my wrist, icicles sinking through my skin. "You expended energy to heal yourself just now. Wouldn't you like to replenish?"

I shiver as frost creeps along my bones, making its way to the energy ball at my core. "What time is it?"

The blue of his eyes shimmers like glacier lakes in the sun. "Only seven."

I slept less than three hours. My focus shifts back to my pillows.

"You don't need a nest if I'm here." He tugs gently on my arm. "Come. I'll cover you."

Lassitude makes my legs weak, and I give in,

crawling beneath the covers. Emil rolls onto his side to create a hollow space for my body to curl against.

The towel around his waist chafes against my thighs, and I reach back to tug on it. "Get rid of this."

"As you wish." He shifts behind me, then the towel soars through the air to land near the doorway. His cold body curls back around mine, his bare thighs pressing against me, the hard lines of his chest against my back. Cool fingers slide beneath the hem of my tank top to skim across my belly, and his lips brush my ear. "You'll absorb more if you take this off."

Grumbling sleepily, I sit up long enough to yank the thin garment over my head and toss it aside before curling back against him. Frost sinks into me from back to ankle, the chilly energy bringing with it the need to sleep.

Emil pulls the blanket over our heads in a simulation of my nest. Light shines through the white down, making it feel like we cuddle inside an igloo.

I sigh with contentment. It's not a nest, but it will definitely do for the next few hours.

Emil paints snowflakes on my stomach, the patterns light as he traces from my lower ribcage to the rim of my belly button. There, he draws a larger snowflake, the complexity lost to my imagination, and I sigh again, my muscles turning to liquid.

What must it be like, to dream in ice?

He shifts, his other arm sliding under my cheek to provide a pillow, and I lean my head back into the curve near his shoulder. His finger dips into my belly button as he completes the pattern, then draws a straight line up to my sternum to draw smaller flakes beneath my breasts. The places he touches tingles, halfway between numb and burning before the energy sinks into my core.

My toes curl as the snowflakes drift downward again and small snow piles build up along the edge of my underwear. I smile as I catch the beginnings of a snowman, small circles that stack on top of each other. The bottom circle hits the elastic of my lace underwear, and Emil's fingers slip beneath to complete the bottom arch. My breath catches, and he pauses, waiting to see if I'll tell him to stop.

But my whole body tingles with awareness, the sleep pushed away with a new desire.

Slowly, Emil traces more snowflakes, his hand sliding deeper beneath the lace until he finds the crest of my mons. Delicate, like the first snow of winter, his touch drifts over my sex, light touches that tease as they melt to the sides to dance at the edges where my legs come together. Liquid heat pools between my thighs, and I press them together to assuage the ache he builds with each almost touch.

Emil drifts back up, his finger light as he traces the outer contour of my folds until he reaches their height. Here, he pauses once more, and the air sticks in my throat as we teeter on the precipice. His touch becomes firmer, the slow slide of an avalanche, as his fingers slip between my folds to find the hard nub of pleasure that waits. My back arches, ass pressing against his hard cock as he circles my clit, then slides lower to find the heat of my core.

He hisses with pleasure, the sound of ice turning to steam, and sinks his fingers into my body. I shiver at the icy intrusion, the feel of his knuckles as he hooks toward my abdomen. Pleasure rushes through me as he massages my inner walls. His thumb delves back to roll against my clit at the same time, and I moan. Reaching back, I clutch his hip, urging him to grind against my ass.

Our quiet pants fill the air as we move together in a push and pull as old as time. Sweat slicks my skin, freezes, then melts to trace runnels over my breasts.

Emil shifts up onto his elbow, and I twist, my arm lifting to pull his mouth to mine. Cold and sweet, his tongue strokes against mine, unhurried as he fills another part of my body. Power trickles across his lips to mine, then flows down my throat, heightening the tension in my core.

I reach down, my hand covering his to urge him faster, but he refuses to be swayed. His strokes stay slow and firm as he drives me to the edge of orgasm.

Frustrated, I nip at his lips, suck on his tongue. I grind my ass against his cock. A cock I want desperately to fill me. I pull my mouth away, panting, "Take off my underwear."

He drifts kisses along my jaw and throat. "No."

I undulate against him. "I want you inside me."

"I'm already inside you." Another finger pushes into my heat.

I groan at the added stretch. "But, I want *more*."

"Shh." His lips come back to mine. "We have time for all of that. There's no need to rush."

His thumb circles my clit again, and my body arches. My muscles clench around his fingers, and he pushes in deep. I roll my hips, riding his fingers as his cock pushes against my ass. His lips catch mine again, power on my tongue, down my throat, and I moan into his mouth as my orgasm hits. My inner muscles clutch his fingers, and I reach down to hold them in place.

With a shaky sigh, he grinds against my ass, then stills, and his cock pulses. Cold cum strikes my lower back, then sinks into my skin, bringing with it a rush of power that makes me come again. I clutch his hand tighter, pressing it to my sex as the orgasm rolls over me in a rush of pleasure. My muscles quiver and my toes curl as I ride the waves.

Slowly, I relax once more and sag against Emil. Breath still uneven, I peer at him over my shoulder, sleepy and languid. "Why'd you give up the chance for sex?"

His brows knit together. "Were you sleeping through what just happened?"

"No, but..." Confusion rolls through me, and I struggle to stay awake. "But I said you could—"

His mouth covers mine in a slow kiss that steals my breath. When his head lifts, he kisses the tip of my nose, then settles behind me once more. "Not everything is about the dick in vagina, Adie."

My mouth drops open in shock at his blunt words.

He brushes my hair aside to kiss the back of my

neck. "I happen to enjoy what we just did immensely. Next time, we'll do it your way."

"I don't–" I lick my lips, unsure in these unfamiliar waters. In my experience, as he put it, *dick in vagina* is what makes sex. I've never been with someone who was okay skipping that part. My voice comes out quiet. "I don't want to pressure you or anything."

Quiet, he strokes my hip, then curls an arm over my waist to tuck me closer. "I get the feeling your experience is..."

He pauses as his hold tightens, and alarm bells go off in my head. I'm not going to appreciate what he says next, and he knows it.

At last, he finishes. "Your experience is narrow."

"Hey, I have a lot of experience!" I wiggle in his hold, but can't turn to face him. "I spent a lot of time in Dreamland sexing it up, for your information."

"Yes. Get the orgasm as fast as you can to get the highest amount of energy." Displeasure fills his voice. "I'm familiar with how most succubi and incubi work."

"There's nothing wrong with that!" I kick his shins, but he only curls tighter around me.

"No, there's not." Despite my obvious anger, he kisses me again. "But there's more out there then what you've been taught. Sex isn't just about food. How full are you right now?"

The question makes me pause, and I focus on the ball of energy at my core. Emil's power rolls around in it, ice threads that mix with the remnants of Kellen's power. But it's not as large as it would be if I fed properly. Which clearly means the dick in vagina thing has more merit.

Frowning, I mutter, "Not full at all."

"But you had fun, right?" His hand splays over my stomach. "And you're not starving."

"I–" A shiver rolls down my spine as my body remembers his fingers inside me. "Yeah, it felt good."

"Sometimes, feeling good is all it needs to be." His fingers skim the elastic of my underwear. "Would you object to repeating what we just did?"

I'd be stupid to turn away that kind of pleasure. "Fine, I get what you're saying."

"But do you understand?" His fingers slide beneath my waistband once more.

"Maybe." Hesitant, I part my legs as my pulse picks up speed once more. "You might need to show me again."

"With pleasure."

(UN)HAUNTING

Eventually, I do fall back asleep, my body spent and filled with enough new energy that I need to digest. When my alarm goes off a few hours later, I drag myself from sleep to find Emil gone. Pillows hug my back in a poor replacement of the ice demon, and his scent still lingers on my sheets, ozone and new snow heavy in the air.

I roll onto my back and stretch. Time to get things done.

Tally offered to take the opening shift again today so I can meet Xander and Reese at the haunted house to deal with that whole mess. They're doing me a favor, and I can't keep them waiting. My eyelids drag, and I force myself to roll out of bed before sleep claims me once more.

After I shower and dress, I stumble downstairs

to the living room and freeze. Tobias's broken chair is missing, an identical replacement in its place. If I didn't know better, I'd think it was the exact same chair.

I wander over to it and touch the leather arm to make sure my mind isn't playing tricks on me. Soft, supple leather warms against my fingertips. When did Kellen get this? I thought we were going shopping together. Am I supposed to just give him money now? While I'm happy to not have this hanging over me anymore, disappointment fills me. I was looking forward to shopping with Kellen.

Leaving the chair for now, I go to the kitchen to grab a quick breakfast before I head out. A coffee cup waits on the counter with a sticky note on top. The familiarity of the scene makes me smile. The guys did this my first day at the bakery, too.

My steps hurry, and I snatch up the pink square. Blocky handwriting fills the paper.

Adie,

You still owe me a chair. I simply brought up the spare from the basement to act as a placeholder until you find the right piece.

· · ·

I fight down a laugh. I can picture Tobias writing this note, annoyed and huffy as he blocks out the letters. Guess I'll still be shopping with Kellen, though we now have a small reprieve. Is this Tobias's way of apologizing for our fight? I need to find an equal way to deliver my apology.

An arrow in the bottom corner prompts me to flip the sticky over. More writing fills the back.

As I tried to tell you yesterday, before you ran off, check with your mentor for that book. I believe he's the most likely of your cousins to have it.

T

Contemplative, I tuck the note into my pocket. I don't want to go out to Landon's. I'm not mentally ready to pull off that metaphysical bandaid. How do I treat him now that I know he's Landrogath the Great Devourer? I'm still shocked he didn't squash me all those times I yelled at him for being a slob.

I lift the to-go cup to my nose and sniff the opening. White chocolate and strawberry. My toes curl in pleasure. Someone saw me eyeing Emil's hot chocolate drawer. Definitely need to find a good way to apologize to Tobias without actually apologizing.

Spinning on one heel, I head for the door.

∼

When I pull up in front of the haunted house, it kills some of my happy mood.

I hoped my memory was bad, and the house wasn't as rundown as I thought it was. No such luck. If anything, the porch looks like it sagged another foot, and more moss covers the roof. How can Kellen rent me this place and *not* call himself a slumlord?

Putting my car in park, I climb out and pick my way over the uneven driveway to the front steps. They creak ominously under my weight. Part of the haunt or rotting wood? I won't know until we dispell this spell-gone-wrong.

The giant hole to who-knows-where seems wider today, too, extending across the porch toward the stairs. If left unattended, will it keep spreading to eventually engulf the whole house? I shake my head at Kellen's irresponsibility; though if it's growing, he can't really throw a board over the top of it. But he has a pocket full of witches at his beck and call.

"Adie, we're here!" a voice calls from the sidewalk.

Speak of the devils.

Eyes still on the hole, I carefully step back before I turn. Xander and Reese skip the driveway to walk across the yellow front lawn. Xander's laptop bag rests at his hip, while Reese carries a large duffle bag on his back.

The dark-haired men look similar enough to be identified as brothers without asking. Their slender, muscular builds and narrow hips move to the same rhythm, a pattern ingrained through a lifetime of knowing each other. That must be so odd, to grow up alongside someone. To share the awkward moments of adolescence, to have someone to fight with and protect.

Demons come into existence through various means, and few lend themselves to the possibility of siblings. Even Tally, whose mother spent time amassing enough power to create two progeny, didn't get to experience the growth cycles with her brother. It would have taken her mother centuries to ready herself for another offspring, by which time

Tally's brother was fully grown and well on his way to amassing power of his own.

"Careful of the steps," I caution as they reach the porch. "I'm not sure how stable they are."

Xander's gaze flicks over the house. "The whole place looks ready to collapse."

"Yeah, I'm not sure how much of this is illusion versus reality." I cross my fingers for the former. I don't want the place to come crashing down on my imps.

Xander takes the stairs first, his feet close to the sides where the boards seem to sag less. Reese, his dual-toned eyes serious, bypasses the two steps altogether, springing over them with a show of strength I never guessed the quiet dreamer possessed.

"Showoff," Xander mutters under his breath.

"Better safe than with a twisted ankle." His attention shifts behind me, and his eyes widen. "I'm not the only one seeing a portal in the porch, am I?"

I stare at him in surprise. "Portal?"

He covers his eyes with one hand. "Oh, god, I'm seeing things again."

"It's not your imagination," Xander quietly reassures him, one hand gripping his shoulder.

"There's a giant hole in the porch with no obvious bottom."

Two of Reese's fingers part to allow him to peek through. "You're not just saying that?"

"Oh, no, there's definitely a bottomless something here," I rush to add. "I just didn't know it was a portal."

I turn to study the edges of the hole, but unlike demon portals, there's no telltale energy flicker. It just looks like a shadowy abyss to me.

Xander crouches at one side, and my hands itch to pull him back to safety. Tally won't forgive me if I lose one of her guys. But Xander's a grown-up, as far as humans are concerned, so I stay put.

He twists to glance back at his brother. "What do you see?"

Reluctant, Reese creeps forward, stopping with a foot of porch between him and the darkness. "There are some symbols." His head tilts. "Runes maybe? But they look soft."

I edge to stand between the two humans and stealthily place one hand near Xander's shoulder, ready to grab him if he shows signs of falling. "Kellen said the cult's spell is unraveling. Maybe that's what you're seeing?"

"Did Kellen say what kind of cult?" Excitement

fills Xander's voice as he reaches for the satchel at his side. "If we know their origin story, undoing this will be easier."

My brows pinch together. "Origin story?"

"Yeah." He pulls his laptop free and opens it, then balances it on one knee. "You know. Where they pulled their mythos from. What god or gods they were trying to worship. Did they make sacrifices? Human? Animal? Every practitioner is different, but they usually start with a pre-existing base and build from there. Very few cults are original in their origin story."

I shake my head, completely lost. "No idea."

"As fascinating as this is," Reese interrupts. "How about we try a simple smudging to clear the air before we get into the more complicated stuff?"

Xander blows out a breath. "Yeah, you're right."

Reluctant, he stands, his laptop balanced on one arm. Curious, I glance over his shoulder to watch as he opens an online app and types *smudging* into a search bar. It pulls up a list of links with descriptors beneath each.

On my other side, Reese shrugs the duffle off his shoulder and sets it on the ground. Unzipping it, he rifles through until he pulls out a thick bundle of herbs that make my nose itch. Ugh. Cedar and sage, with a hint of frankincense.

Reese gives me an apologetic glance. "You might want to step back."

"A little herb's not going to banish me." But I move closer to the railing, anyway. That thing stinks, and he hasn't even lit it yet.

Reese pulls a zippo from his pant pocket and flicks it open with a metallic *clink*. After a couple tries, the flame lights and checks with his brother. "You have the right one pulled up?"

"I think so." Xander concentrates on the laptop screen, his mouth forming silent words as he reads over the spell.

Human magic is a slippery thing, unnatural to modern language, and a wrong word can change the entire outcome. Or so I've heard. I'm too young to have dealt with witches, but Julian tells good stories when he's nostalgic for the old days when demons were allowed to hunt witches freely.

At last, Xander nods, and Reese lights the smudge stick. Thick white smoke plumes outward, unnaturally heavy as he circles the giant hole. I clutch the railing and take shallow breaths through my mouth as I attempt to not breathe the dense fog.

Once he makes a full circle counterclockwise,

Xander begins to chant. It holds a lilting quality that speaks to the songs of the ancients, the slippery words almost legible to my ears. But they slide past my ability to understand and sink into the smoke, crafting symbols from the fog. Reese continues his circuit, his steps slow and steady as he watches the hole.

On his third pass, the tension in his face eases, the corners of his mouth twitching with a suppressed smile. Their magic must be working.

On the fifth pass, the hole begins to close, but slowly. Too slowly, if Reese's sudden concern is anything to go by. The smudge stick in his hand is already burned halfway down, and his eyes flick to his duffle bag. He can't break the circuit, or they'll have to start over.

Reluctant, I give them a wide berth as I walk to the duffle bag and crouch next to it. Spell crafting paraphernalia fills the black canvas. Some I recognize from trophies Julian showed me while my eyes slide past others, unable to focus on them directly.

A small sack lays in the center, the ends of more smudge sticks visible. I pinch one and pull it free, ignoring the tingle in my fingers as I stand. I walk back to the guys, and on Reese's next pass, I hand it over. He gives me a relieved smile and tucks it into his back pocket as he continues past.

I settle back at my place next to the railing, watching in fascination as the porch knits itself back together. The boards left in its place look sturdy and new like they never broke in the first place.

At last, the final bit of darkness disappears. Reese makes a couple more laps, just to be safe, before Xander falls quiet.

"That was great, guys!" I straighten and rub my palms together. "Hopefully, the rest of the house is that easy."

"Yeah, easy," Xander says dryly as he shuts his laptop. He rolls his neck to the sound of vertebrae popping.

Reese stubs out the remainder of the second smudge stick before he walks to the duffle and digs out a couple bottles of water. He passes one to his brother, who downs half the bottle in a few fast gulps, and holds the other up to me in question.

I wave it away. I didn't do much, and I don't want to risk needing the bathroom while we're here. The one glance inside I took was enough to scare me away from putting my bare butt on any surfaces inside without a thorough cleaning. Who knows what would crawl up there?

"Do you need a break before we go into the house?" I ask as Reese tucks the empty water bottles back into the bag and hefts it over his shoulder.

Do human witches lose energy the same way demons do? Or do they pull their magic from somewhere else? While the ones Julian hunted enhanced their gifts with the use of demon body parts, I didn't see any of those in Reese's bag, and I don't think the clay discs they all wear count.

Laptop tucked under one arm, Xander rolls his shoulders and jogs in place a couple times. "We should be good." He clears his throat loudly. "Reese, we might need to switch if we have to do this for every room."

"Yeah, okay." The corners of Reese's eyes pinch with unhappiness, but he squares his shoulders "Let's get this done."

I dig the keys out of my pocket and hug the exterior wall of the house to reach the front door. While the porch now looks sound, I can't bring myself to test the surface yet. Reese and Xander show no such caution as they walk across it, their steps echoing on the hollow underside.

I flick the lion head knocker to make it clunk against the metal plate. "Look familiar?"

"Ugh, yes." Xander shudders while Reese reaches out and strokes the brass animal's ugly snout.

"Who's a good guardian?" Reese whispers, so quiet I don't believe he meant for us to hear.

As I slide the key into the lock and turn it, a brief flicker of red fills the lion's eyes, then fades away. Huh. Creepy.

I shove the door open and stare at the dingy foyer. "Okay, so. As soon as we get to the stairs"—I make a so-so gesture with my hand to show it's an approximation—"the door's going to slam shut and things are going to get haunty. I've already done this run once, so I know how to turn it off fast. You guys just hang tight up here until the lights turn back on. Any questions?"

Reese shakes his head as his curious gaze skips around what he can see of the interior.

Xander grips his laptop tighter. "Are we talking ghosts here?"

"Um, more like shadows." I walk over the threshold and wait for them to follow before venturing farther into the house. I don't want to be stuck in here alone. That would defeat the purpose of bringing them. "Oh, and lots of insects."

"Spiders?" Xander's voice squeaks.

"Yeah. And rats." I shrug, unconcerned. "Or, some other tiny critter with claws."

"Maybe we should try to smudge the entire house from the outside, first," Xander whispers.

"Too late!" I reach the hallway next to the stairs, and the door slams shut.

Darkness surrounds us, followed by the sharp scrape of nails against the walls. An eerie, hollow voice growls, "What new treat has ventured into our home?"

"Oh, fuck," Xander mutters.

"Awesome," Reese whispers.

"Be right back!" Shrugging out of my hoodie, I drape it over the stair rail and unfurl my wings.

My feathers rustle, and Xander lets out another groaned curse before I hyper-speed away, aiming straight for the basement.

I vault through the doorway, high-five the mysteriously swinging lightbulb, and land on the wall right next to the narrow window. I knock it open to let the beams of light stream in, then bounce over the waving tentacles, grab the mirror under the stairs, and slam it into place. Sunshine shoots around the room.

"You will not defeat me!" the nightmare howls, and a cloud of black rushes toward me.

"Boom!" I tip the mirror, enjoying the lightsaber action as it cuts the monster in half.

Haunt over.

Leaving the mirror in place, I hyper-speed back to the foyer, where I find Xander huddled behind Reese. Both men blink in the sudden brightness cast by the overhead chandelier.

I pull my phone from my pocket and check the time. "I'm not sure how long we have before the haunt resets itself, so you might want to get to work."

As if to dislodge the memory of spiders, Xander shakes himself all over, then whips his laptop open once more. Muttering, he walks around. "Reception in here sucks."

"This is why I keep saying we should have a paper copy," Reese points out calmly as he settles his duffle bag on the ground.

"You offering to lug that around?" Xander demands as he scrolls quickly through a list of links.

"You could keep it with your laptop, as a backup." Reese's gaze shifts to me, and I try not to shiver as the slash of brown across his pupil gives him an otherworldly aura. "Xander's the best of us. If we had a full coven, he'd be our leader."

"You're not supposed to talk about that," Xander

mutters, but he sounds distracted. "Haunting. Spiders. Dark shadows..."

Curious, I walk closer to Reese and eye his stuffed bag of tricks. "How long have you guys been doing this?"

His focus shifts and he pulls out a leather bag that clanks with the sound of rocks rolling together. "About five months? I think? Time's a little hard for me sometimes."

"Six months," Xander responds absently. Despite his distraction, he seems amazingly attuned to his brother. "Not the stones, Reese. Those are for forest spirits."

Grinning, Reese puts the leather bag away and pulls out a bundle of feathers.

"We're not in the mountains." Irritation fills Xander's voice. "Stop messing around."

Reese leans closer to me, his voice conspiratorial. "He doesn't like to admit he's attuned to the magic. He probably doesn't even need the website."

"We're not having this argument again." Xander stomps over to us. "Going off book leads to bad things happening." He crouches, shoves a hand into the duffle, and pulls out a bag of white powder. He shoves it into Reese's hands. "Start barring the doorways."

Reese tips his head at Xander as his brother marches away, as if he just proved his point. Which he did. I assumed Reese, as the fae-touched one, would be the most powerful of the four. Given more time and room to grow, Kellen's pet witches could be a terrifying weapon.

Does he know the danger he's messing with if they turn on him? On us?

I watch as Reese circles the room, carefully pouring a thin, unbroken line of white sand in front of every opening, including the foot of the stairs. When he finishes, he sets the bag next to his duffle and digs out a fat piece of chalk from one of the side pockets. With a quick check of the perimeter, he chooses a spot a little to the left of the chandelier and crouches once more. With fluid movements, he chalks a circle onto the floor, then a second one around it.

Xander stands near the front door, his back to his brother, when he instructs, "No angelscrit."

Reese pauses, chalk against the floor. "Are you sure?"

"The spell's already soft, no reason to expend more than we need to." He turns, his gaze unfocused as he glances in my general direction. "Don't break the salt lines."

Confused, I stare at him, a little unnerved. "What?"

The house plummets back into darkness. "What new treat has ventured into our home?"

With a sigh, I hyper-speed back to the basement, hopping over the white line that bars the hall. That must be the salt Xander warned me about. I make it to the basement, dispel the haunt, and arrive back in the foyer as the lights return. Somehow, in that time, Reese filled the space between the inner and outer circles with slashing marks my eyes refuse to focus on. Xander now stands at the center, laptop in hand.

I check the clock on my phone. "That was fifteen minutes."

Reese chews his lip in worry. "Not a lot of time."

"Then, we better make this fast." Xander looks at me without really seeing. "You might want to stand on the other side of the salt. I'm not sure what this will do to a demon."

"No problem." I hop onto the bottom stair and sit, fascinated.

I've seen room purifications before, and the smudging on the porch wasn't much different, aside from the spellcraft Xander added in. But this kind of ritual is new territory.

Reese tucks the chalk into his back pocket and settles on the ground in front of Xander, his legs folded neatly in front of him. With his hands close together, he leans forward to press his fingers to the outer chalk ring and closes his eyes.

A faint, blue glow spreads around the circle and streaks inward, highlighting the harsh lines of the spell. As much as I want to watch, my eyes won't stay on the pair, and I give up, focusing on the salt line in front of the stairs.

Xander's voice slides past my ears, tickling at my senses, and light flickers in my peripheral vision. I turn my head toward them, but my eyes stick to the salt line, which makes my head ache. I want to look so bad, but my body won't let me.

After five minutes, the light fades, and my eyes instantly snap to the brothers. Xander crouches in his circle, his body folded over his laptop, while Reese sprawls on the floor. Both pant quietly.

I grip the baluster beside me. "Is it safe now?"

Reese lifts his hand in a limp wave.

I jump back over the salt line. "Are you guys okay?"

"Yeah, this one was just hard because of the vaulted ceiling," Xander gasps.

"Will you have to do this in each room?" I check the clock. We have another four minutes before the haunt kicks back in.

Reese rolls onto his side, then pushes himself to sit up. "This might be a two-day project."

"No, we can do it in one," Xander protests.

"Maybe if we had Slater and Jax with us." Reese rubs chalk dust onto his jean-clad thighs. "I don't know how many circles I can power in a row."

"If we were better, we could put the whole house in a circle and exorcise it all at once."

"That's how you burn out."

Xander's eyes narrow. "I know. That's why we're doing it one room at a time."

My attention bounces back and forth between them as they argue. "If it takes a couple days, or longer, that's fine. I don't need to move my people until the end of next week."

Xander scrubs his hands over his face. "This sucks."

"I'm sorry." My shoulders sag at his exhausted expression. "I didn't realize how much this would take from you guys. I should never have asked this of you."

"No, it's not you." Reese reaches into the circle and raps his knuckles on the top of his brother's head. "Stop it. Just because you mastered coding when you were twelve doesn't mean everything will come that naturally. Give it time."

"But this should be easier." Xander grabs his laptop and thrusts to his feet. "I know what I need to do. It shouldn't be this *hard*."

Oh. It's one of those types of situations. I rock on my heels for a moment and watch as Xander scuffs his shoe around the chalk circle to break up the words. His actions hold frustration and anger, his movements jerky.

I come to a stop. "You know, I'm seventy-nine years old."

They look at me in surprise, and I purse my lips. These are humans, but revealing this still makes my skin crawl at the show of weakness. "I don't know how much you know about my kind, but we're not usually let on the human plane before we're a hundred. I was...impatient. And bullheaded. I refused to listen to my mentor. I took a corporeal form before I finished amassing the correct level of power."

Slowly, I let my wings unfurl from their hiding place and spread the feathers. "My wings are small, and they have no color. I can't read the demon language or return to Dreamland because, in my impatience, I broke something inside myself."

Their eyes move between me and my wings, and I force myself to stay exposed so they can fully take in the tiny feathers that can barely lift me from the ground.

"Like you, I know how to fix myself, but it will take time." Unable to stand it any longer, I pull my wings back to their hiding place along my spine.

"Amassing power takes time. Skill takes time. Knowledge is the easiest part of this sort of process. But it doesn't matter how smart you are, how much you know. You have to keep practicing, then practice some more. Push yourself, but don't break whatever's inside you that lets you do this." I sweep a hand to the hazy chalk circle. "You're human, and humans adapt quickly. You'll be able to circle an entire house in no time. But before that, we'll take this one room at a time until we're done, okay?"

Xander hangs his head. "You're right. I know you're right. It's just frustrating."

His frustration finds an echo inside me. I feel the exact same way. Knowing I need to go slow and amass the power here that I should have gained while in Dreamland makes me itch with impatience.

But there's nothing I can do about it besides continue to focus forward instead of wallowing in what I should have done in the past.

Reese studies me intently, his dual-toned eyes seeming to see past my physical body, and I fold my arms over my stomach, a little uncomfortable.

His gaze shifts up, to my forehead, and he smiles. "I think you'll get sorted out soon, too. So, don't give up."

Confused, I rub a hand on my forehead. "What do you mean?"

"I've seen other succubi. Well, incubi, technically. They all had a string linking here"–he points to my stomach, right over my ball of energy–"to here." His hand moves up to my forehead, and my eyes cross as I follow the motion. "Your string is broken, but it's longer than it was when we first met. Whatever you're doing to fix yourself, it's working."

Surprised, I close my eyes and focus in on myself. A string? I felt something like that when my cousins threw me that housewarming party. When we all danced together, I saw it within myself. But then evil Cassandra arrived and everything went to shit. I try to find it again, imagining some kind of permanent thread of energy extending from my center.

"Um, Adie?" Xander's hesitant voice disrupts my inner search, and my eyes snap open once more to find the rooms leading off from the foyer pitched into darkness.

"Right. We still have more to do for the day." I bounce on my toes with excitement. "I'll be right back."

As I hyper-speed back to the basement, I feel like this time, I'm conquering more than just the nightmare in the house. If Reese is right, and I believe he is because the fae-touched see differently than humans or demons, then maybe I won't be broken for much longer.

Now, I just needed to face a boogeyman and demand some answers.

Step On My Grave

When I arrive at the bakery, the imps give me a wide berth. Can't say that I blame them. The smoke from the smudging sticks to my clothes, and despite standing outside the salt lines, I can't help but feel like the human magic clings to me in some way. I wanted a shower, but clearing the ground level took longer than expected, so I came straight to work to give everyone their first break of the day.

Unlike the imps, Tally shows no hesitation as she bounces over to greet me, her eyes bright with excitement. "How did it go?"

"Pretty good, but it's going to take a few days. It's a pretty big house, and we get interrupted every fifteen minutes." I shrug out of my hoodie and hang it on the hook in the hall, then pull on my chef jacket. "Anything happen here I need to know about?"

She clasps her hands in front of her chest. "Nope, the store is running smoothly!"

I pull an elastic band from my pocket and twist my hair into a bun, fixing it in place. "Okay, I'm going to check on Torch real fast, then I can work the front counter while you and the imps take a break."

"Is something wrong with Torch?" She twists to stare back into the kitchen. "He's baking at the perfect level of heat."

"No, I just want to say hi and make sure Jesse didn't sneak more bocote wood into his bowl." Despite my warning, I might need to hide the expensive pellets in a better spot, or Torch will stop eating the cheaper stuff.

"Ah, Jesse does like to spoil him." She leans closer, her voice low. "Have you spoken to the imp about the risks of not choosing a form? I do not know why this one is so resistant."

"It just hasn't seen a shape it likes." I shrug the niggles of worry away. "Give it time. Until then, Jesse just needs to stay in the kitchen."

"I suppose." Spinning away, Tally heads for the two-way door. "I'll check the display cases to see if we are low on any flavors."

"Thank you!" I call as she disappears.

As I walk to the wall of ovens, Iris rubs her nose and turns away. One of the pinwheels I hid around the store makes jagged peaks beneath her hairnet. Did they already find the other hidden prizes? Will I need to hide more tonight? Maybe I should look online for shiny, bulk items. Going to the store will get expensive if I'm not careful.

I crouch next to the oven and grab the pair of heat-resistant gloves that sit in a basket off to one side, purchased after Torch melted the last pair of tongs. They make my fingers thick and unwieldy when I wear them, but they stand up to Torch's fire so I count the discomfort worth it.

When I pop open the little hatch on the side of one oven, heat radiates out, lifting the fine strands of hair next to my face. I close my eyes, inhaling the dry air, and wait for fear to follow. But my instincts to run remain dormant. No danger here, despite the fact Torch almost killed me when he briefly grew too big for his ovens.

Is the intent behind the action really what triggers my fear? But Tobias doesn't intend to hurt me, does he?

Torch comes running from the far side of the

oven on stubby legs, his flame turning blue when he spots me. He waves little arms in the air in greeting, and I reach into the oven to gently scoop him out. Aww, how could I ever fear the small ignes demon?

He flickers through the range of fire, orange, yellow, blue, white, and even purple. Somehow, I think he's asking me about my day and telling me he's pleased to see me.

"My day's been good. How about you?" I gently squeeze his rounded belly, and he turns blue with happiness. "Are you baking all the cakes to perfection?"

He flickers and pats at his stomach.

"Yes, you always do such a good job." I bring him closer until the heat of his fire makes my skin tight. Still no fear. Even if he burned me now, I'd still love him.

When I wiggle my fingers through the flames on top of his head, he rolls around in my palm, flickering from red to yellow.

"Okay, we should both get back to work."

Sprawled on my palm, he pats his round belly again.

"Oh, you think I should give you more pellets?" I shift him to the side and peer into the hatch at his food basket. Small, dark brown balls of wood line his tray. "You have plenty in there."

Pat, pat on the belly.

"Is this how you con Jesse into the good wood?" I pinch him once more. "You stop that or no more treats."

Gently, I set him back inside his hatch. Instantly, he rolls to his feet and goes to the food bowl. He plucks out a pellet and holds it out to me.

I shake my head. "No, thank you, I'm not hungry."

Flickering, he shoves the pellet into his own stomach. His flames brighten for a moment, then settle back to a steady glow.

I reach for the door, ready to close it. "Have a good rest of the day, Torch."

He pauses, one stumpy arm in the food bowl again, and waves as I lock the latch.

Slowly, I pull off the gloves and return them to the basket. I'm glad I'm not afraid of Torch, but confused on why I can't make the same logical leap for Tobias. Maybe he just smells too much like Domnall?

While all three smell like fire, Torch has never once reminded me of a blazing forest. He doesn't emit any ash, either. He's a clean-burning, little demon.

Hands on my thighs, I push to my feet, ready to relieve Tally at the front.

Basking in the happiness of humans will help take my mind off the problems I can't fix right now.

∽

At seven, Tally restocks the display case, then leaves for the night, Jax by her side. I force her to take two boxes of cupcakes with her, worried Xander and Reese need to refuel themselves after all the magic they expended earlier. They refused to accept payment for their services, but they won't refuse food. And sugar's a quick and dirty energy kick. It will perk them up, then crash them hard. Hopefully hard enough to sleep in late tomorrow.

Kelly bustles around the front of the shop, a tray in one hand as he collects mugs and empty plates, then wipes down the tables to ready them for the next customer. Behind the espresso machine, Martha runs steam through the wands and cleans the coffee grounds from the counter in front of her station.

The shop runs smoothly, now, with everyone

settled into their preferred roles, and the imps seem happy with the work. A sparkle ball falls from Kelly's pocket and bounces under the table he works on.

Unaware, he lifts his bucket and moves to the next table. Down the counter, the steam cuts off. Martha creeps around the display case, darts forward, and snatches the blue puff up, stuffing it into her apron pocket as she makes a quick escape.

I smile at the imps' antics. Why did I ever think mischief imps were a bad idea?

Feeling a little bad for Kelly's lost treasure, I unlock the drawer under the register and pull out a precious, flower-topped pen, setting it in the cup next to the signing pad. I can't outright give it to him. If I do, it won't slake his mischief urges. But I can make the prizes easy to find.

A new customer steps up to the counter with a toddler balanced on her hip. "Hey, I'd like a pink rose and a bumblebee mini for here, please."

As Martha pulls plates from the back counter, tongs already in hand, I ring up the items. "Would you like anything to drink with that?"

"Umm..." Her gaze moves up to the signboard over my head. "A milk and a hibiscus tea, please."

"Hot or cold on the tea?"

She bounces the kid higher. "Cold, please."

I add the drinks, tell her the total, then wait as she juggles the child to find her purse and dig out her credit card. At last, she passes it over, and I run it through the reader, then hold the receipt so she can sign with only one hand. "I'll have someone bring you your order."

With an expression of relief, she moves off to one of the booths where she can more easily trap her kid.

As I turn to the next customer, a shiver of apprehension rolls through me, and the smile fades from my face.

The elderly lady in front of me freezes, then peers over her shoulder before turning back. "Dear, are you alright?"

The question snaps me back to reality, and I focus on her with a sheepish look. "I had a sudden chill."

She nods knowingly. "Someone just stepped on your grave."

Shocked, I blink at her. "Excuse me?"

"You know the old saying." Her lips purse, the wrinkles around her mouth deepening. "When there's an unexplainable chill, someone's walking on your grave."

"Oh," I say weakly. "I don't think I've heard that one before."

She huffs. "Must be too young."

I'm pretty sure I have a decade on her but ignore the comment. "What can I get for you?"

My body registers her order, going through the motions of ringing her up, but white noise fills my ears. Danger lurks nearby. The same feeling I sensed here before, the same that followed me and Slater, then me and Tobias. Domnall must be near. But why?

The guys said he wouldn't need to dump more energy so soon, that he doesn't regenerate the way they do.

A fine tremor shakes my hand as I take the boxed cupcake from Martha and pass it to the customer. As she walks toward the exit, movement in the window catches my eye. A dark figure stares into the shop, his face obscured by the frosted imprint of Boo's Boutique Bakery.

Fear trembles down my legs, but I square my shoulders. This ends now. I won't let Domnall terrorize me any longer. "Martha, please have Iris cover the register. I'll be right back"

"Yes, master."

I let the honorific slide, too focused on the

hovering menace at my door. The bell tinkles, a happy sound as I shove my way out of the shop. When I turn to the window, though, I find the sidewalk empty. A flicker of movement near the alley draws my attention, and the fear turns into full-on panic. Bad things happen when I meet dark figures in alleys.

My hands curl into fists. I'm prepared this time. I have hyper-speed, strength, and a belly full of ice and lightning. He won't ambush me again.

I march forward on shaky legs and turn into the shadow-covered alley. The sudden darkness blinds me for a moment, and my breath catches. Then, my eyes adjust, and I see the empty alley, sunlight at the opposite end beckoning me to the rear parking lot. How did Domnall move so fast? Is he running? Is he trying to lure me to a more secluded area to gain the upper hand?

I hesitate to venture farther. I want to confront him, but I'm not completely stupid. If I follow him to a location of his choice, he'll take the advantage. No, I need to cast a lure of my own.

Decision made, I turn back to the sunlit street when an acrid smell reaches me. My nostrils flare, dragging in the sharp odor of spray paint. Was this not Domnall at all but that hoodlum returning to tag my shop again?

Relief and anger war with each other as I walk deeper into the alley. Sure enough, ugly black lines cover the wall next to my door, still wet and dripping black paint. A larger, mirror image of the first tag, with circles and harsh lines. Looking at them makes my head ache, and I rub my temples. Ugh, I haven't even painted over the last one yet. Luckily, no one seemed to notice the slightly darker paint on the door or they would have mentioned it.

Tugging off my chef's coat, I rub at the new graffiti, smearing the black paint into the old bricks. This one won't vanish so easily, but at least I can wipe it away enough that it won't be recognizable by any gang.

Do we even have gangs in this neighborhood? This is ridiculous.

I scrub hard and sniff back the tears that sting my nose. I faced off with demons of destruction, I defeated a haunted house. I will not be brought down by street punks.

At last, I stop wiping at the mark. It won't get any better without paint thinner. I'll stop at the hardware store tomorrow after I meet with Xander and Reese again. Sweat trickles down my temples, and I lift a hand, only to see black on my palms, too. Frustrated, I use my shoulder to catch the moisture, then find a clean patch on my coat to cover my stained hand before I open the door.

I walk straight to the bathroom and stuff the ruined garment in the trash, then turn the water on as hot as it will go and scrub until the paint disappears and my skin turns pink from the heat.

Finished, I dry my hands off and grab a fresh chef's coat from the pantry before I return to the front of the shop. Iris has the cash register handled, so I check the stock in the case. The bumblebee bites are low. Parents love the smaller size for their kids, and I like to see their teeth turn green from the frosting. Win, win for everyone.

I pat Iris on the arm as I head back to the kitchen to frost up a new batch.

The Big Bad

"Have a good night everyone!" I call as Philip herds the imps into the back of the HelloHell Delivery van.

He slams the door shut, gives me a quick salute, then runs around to the driver's side as I turn to my much smaller sedan. My too small sedan.

How am I going to cart the imps back and forth in this thing?

As the largest, Kelly will need to take the front seat. Can Iris, Martha, and Perry wedge into the back, with Jesse on someone's lap? What if the cops pull me over? How do I explain Jesse's gray skin?

I need a bigger car. Maybe an SUV with tinted windows.

The one time I peeked into the garage at home to see if there was room for my car, I found it full. Five vehicles dominated the large space, two draped in cloth. One was big enough to possibly be an SUV, but which of the guys does it belong to and what will I give up to drive it?

I put those thoughts on the back-burner, too tired to give it serious attention. I have time to figure out that aspect of being the imps' new contractor.

Right now, all I want is to go home to bed. But the sticky note in my pocket reminds me I have other duties to complete, so I climb into my little sedan and head out of the city.

Thirty minutes later, I pull into the drive-thru at the Bucket-O-Wings. The giant rooster sign shines orange light through my windshield as I roll down my window.

The microphone crackles, and a nasal voice drones, "Bucket-O-Wings, where life tastes better deep fried. How may I help you?"

Leaning out the window, I shout, "I'd like two twelve-piece buckets, six biscuits, and a large potato salad, please."

I hadn't told Landon I was coming; the least I can do is arrive with his favorite chicken dinner.

"Crispy, extra-crispy, or crispy-supreme?"

"Crispy-supreme." I read over the menu. "Do you have any of the strawberry cheesecakes left?"

"We have apple or custard pies, ma'am."

Of course not. They never have them. I don't know why they're even on the menu. I sigh. "That's it for me."

"That will be fifty-one twenty-three at the first window."

I pull forward and wait behind a green minivan for my turn. When I pull up to the window, I see the same pimple-faced teenager from when I crashed on Landon's couch after being evicted. He takes my money, minus the boob gawking. Guess my tank top and hoodie aren't as enticing as the lace bra I pulled up in last time.

He barely glances at me as he shoves the three large bags of food through the window, then leans out to peer at the cars behind me. Annoyed, I put the paper sacks in the passenger seat and pull back onto the road.

The smell of fried chicken makes my mouth water, and I suffer through the torment of the next five minutes to Landon's house.

When I pull into the driveway, the one-story house looks exactly as I left it. I grab the food and head for the front door, juggling the bags to get it open. Water bottles cascade across the front hall in a hollow tide of plastic. I kick them out of the way and bump the door closed with my ass. The empty crates and stacks of pizza boxes grew since my sleepover, and I turn sideways to shuffle down the hall.

"Landon, you here?" I call.

For once, the house stays silent. Usually, the rattle of electronic gunfire or Landon's voice as he hollers at his online teammates fills the air. The lack of noise makes me nervous.

"Landon?"

The hallway spills me into the kitchen, where bright lights dance stars across my eyes. Jewel-toned butterflies erupt into the air to flutter around my head. The room past the kitchen lays in darkness, Landon's giant, flat-screen TV shut off.

"Landon, you here?" My mentor is *always* here. In the last ten years, I've known him to leave the house a handful of times.

My steps slow as I approach the next room. Please don't let this be the day I find my mentor mummified on the couch, his game controller clutched in his bony claws. My heart races as I spot the thin lump on the couch. Against a pillow, his white hair stands out stark in the darkness.

"Landon?" My voice wobbles as I creep forward.

Please don't be a husk. I'll come here more often,

clean his house, and bring him food. I can't lose him right now.

He snorts and rolls onto his side, the blanket sliding from his shoulders. Relief turns my knees to jelly, and I sag against the couch. Where his hole-riddled t-shirt rides up, it exposes healthy muscle. Thank goodness. He must be on his monthly hunt.

Tiptoeing, I set the food on the coffee table among the piles of empty water bottles then creep back to the kitchen where he keeps a box of recycling bags under the sink. I shake open one of the blue plastic bags as quietly as possible and begin to load it with the water bottles from the hall. One bag turns into ten, and I prop the front door open to pile them in the driveway. There's a service I call to come to collect them.

From the garage, I find the paper yard waste bags, stack the pizza boxes inside, then add them to the opposite side of the driveway for the yard people to pick up.

For all his age, Landon's house isn't that large. It only has two bedrooms, and he never uses the master, spending all of his time in the living room. The other still holds the twin-size bed I used to sleep in, the butterfly quilt tucked down on one side as if awaiting my return.

Sun peeks over the horizon by the time I finish cleaning the front half of the house. I kept my eyes open the entire time, but found no books. Not surprising. Landon doesn't even buy gaming manuals, calling them instructions for the weak. He either passes or fails through his own skill and takes ridiculous pride in it.

Maybe that's why I never considered going to the library to self-educate myself. Everything comes so naturally to Landon I assumed the same would happen for me, too.

Recycling bags in hand, I creep into the living room, which I left for last to give Landon the longest time possible to stock up energy. The room now holds the scent of stale grease, the fried chicken gone cold long ago.

As I lean over the table, my toe kicks a water bottle, and it bounces against the couch. Landon's eyelids flutter, and a thin band of yellow shines through. "Boo?"

"Don't wake up," I whisper. "Keep feeding."

"Mmm." Fitful, he rolls until his back faces me, then pats his shoulder in search of the quilt.

I drop the bag, circle the table to pick the blanket off the ground, and drape it over him. He releases a long sigh and settles back into sleep. Not wanting to wake him again, I resist the urge to comb his hair back from his face. It's getting long and shows monarch yellow at the tips. I'll need to trim it the next time I come to visit.

The thought forms naturally, with none of the recalcitrance I felt before. Landon may be one of the big bads of our kind, but he's also the gruff, often forgetful, man who raised me. The same one who showed me the good side of humans, their unique fragility that made me unwilling to hurt them. He wasn't the best teacher, but he also supported me when I left Dreamland early. Anyone else would have destroyed my newly formed body to force me back as soon as they discovered I couldn't transition on my own.

Landon let me be me, big mistakes and all.

Clearing the rest of the table, I set his controller on top of the bag of fried chicken to make sure he notices the mortal food when he wakes, then walk back to the kitchen.

I crouch in front of the sink to put the cleaning supplies away and make a mental list to bring more wood cleaner next time. The recycling and compost are picked up, but dust filters through the air in a thick enough cloud that my throat hurts from breathing it. I'd open a window to air out the house, but then Landon's precious butterflies might escape.

Standing, I turn and eye the table. Flower pots cover the surface and feeders hang from the chandelier. Emil sat at that table when he came to offer me their stupid contract a second time. He brought with him my abandoned shirt from the nightclub. I lost my shoes that night, too, and now spot them on the floor. How did I miss them before?

Oh, yeah, I was in too much of a hurry to flee the ice demon's clutches.

I walk to the table and bend to scoop them up, then freeze as I spot the book that props up one leg of the table. No. Freaking. Way.

Couching, I lift the table and slide the book free. Years of potting dirt cake the cover, but I make out demonic symbols on the spine. Just to make sure, I get my phone out and check the picture I took of the title. The symbols look like they match. The ones on the book creep together, and my eyes cross to keep them in focus. Okay, they look close enough that I'll give it a shot.

Eager to get this over with, I tuck my dress shoes under one arm and head for the door. The frame shimmers, power prickles along my skin, and I stumble into the hall of doors at the library.

"Fuck!" I try to halt my forward momentum and twist to the side so I don't face-plant into the opposite wall. "Give a girl a little warning, will you?"

The hag's cackle fills the hall and rattles the panes in the doorframes. "Not my fault you can't see a portal before you walk through it."

Lesson learned from last time, I shove myself upright and head toward the front desk at a normal pace. The journey will take as long as it takes, no reason to blow all my energy this time.

The journey takes less than five seconds and gives me a sneaking suspicion the Librarian's impatience has a lot to do with the length of the hall of portals.

Today, the library sports a torture room feel with a metal grate floor and disturbingly sharp implements dangling from the shelves. The tang of pennies hangs in the air, and my wings rustle a warning of danger.

Behind her desk, the hag waits with her hands folded, a wrinkly statue of ugliness. She'd look right at home in a garden, scaring away the crows.

I stride up to her desk and drop the book in front of her. "There you go. We done here?"

Her head swivels to the side. "Aren't you curious at all?"

"Not really." At this point, I don't even care about the book she offered in trade. I just want to go home and get a few hours of sleep before my day starts again.

"You really should be." One hand covers the book, her claws scratching away at the embedded grime.

"Why?" I scowl. "You know I can't read it anyway."

"Ah, but you know people who can." Dirt flakes away to reveal a symbol etched on the cover and my blood turns cold. She grins, displaying a sharp line of pointed teeth. "Ah, now I have your attention."

Reaching for the book, I brush more of the dirt away. A black circle filled with jagged lines sinks into the cover as if burned there. "Hey, this is the same as the graffiti some punk keeps spraying on my door."

"Not graffiti." She clicks her tongue in disapproval. "A warning. You, baby succubus, have been marked."

My head jerks up. "Marked? Marked how?"

"The Hunters are back, and you've caught their attention." Her voice becomes a quiet croon. "Poor, baby succubus, struggling and low on power. The perfect demon to break down for parts."

I jerk my hand away from the book as if burned. "How do I stop them?"

"It's time to circle your wagons, Adeline Boo Pond. Tie the demons of destruction to your side, get those little witches to cast their protection, and seek out He Who Devours." She shoves the book at me. "Fill yourself with power. It's time to grow up or be destroyed."

The library ripples around me and morphs into the office of K&B Financials. Behind his desk, Emil looks up in surprise. For one disorienting moment, the hag's image overlaps him, blacking out his eyes.

Then the library fades completely.

She didn't even use a doorway this time, which makes my skin crawl. I clutch the dirty book to my chest. The hag officially scares me more than any other demon I've met.

Emil rises, concern and confusion clear on his face. "Adie? What's going on?"

My heart pounds in my throat. "Call Tobias and Kellen. We need to talk."

In my head, the words play on loop. *The Hunters are back.*

And they want to harvest me.

Succubus Hunted
The (un)Lucky Succubus Book 4

The Hunters marked Adie's bakery. Now they plan to capture and harvest her body to use in their dark magic. Demons are supposed to be the boogeymen in this world, so why are these evil witches so much worse?

The Librarian told her to gather her people close, that she would need all of her resources to survive the coming battle, but her sexy demons seem determined to keep her out of it. How can she protect her people and herself if she's put in the corner and told to wait?

As a demon who loves to bake and a succubus who refuses to feed on humans, is there a place for Adie in this world? And what price will she pay to find it?

ABOUT THE AUTHOR

L.L. Frost lives in the Pacific Northwest and graduated from college with a Bachelor's in English. She is an avid reader of all things paranormal and can frequently be caught curled up in her favorite chair with a nice cup of coffee, a blanket, and her Kindle.

When not reading or writing, she can be found trying to lure the affection of her grumpy cat, who is very good at being just out of reach for snuggle time.

To stay up to date on what L.L. Frost is up to, join her newsletter, visit her website, or follow her on social media!

www.llfrost.com

Printed in Great Britain
by Amazon